HE SMELLED SOMETHING SUSPICIOUS . . .

Jackie smiled brightly at the manager of the dog-training academy. "Tell me—if I were to sign Jake up for a class here, I think I would really have to see the grounds. Could you show me around?"

"We do our obedience training right out front there." He gestured toward the large field that separated the kennel operation from the house.

"Oh." Jackie bit her lip. "But what if Jake needs to spend the night? I'll have to inspect the dogs' living quarters, I think, before—"

"Look, Mrs. Walsh. *If* that's your name." Tom Mann had risen suddenly from his chair, and he stood glowering at Jackie. He raised his voice and pointed an accusing finger at her. "I don't want to be rude, but we've had an awful lot of reporters snooping around out here. Some of them pretended they wanted to have their dogs trained. They were a *little* bit better at it than you are—because at least they brought their own dogs with them, not some rent-a-dog from the nearest kennel." He gestured sharply at Jake.

Jake looked solemnly at Mann. . . .

DOG COLLAR CRIME

MELISSA CLEARY

BERKLEY PRIME CRIME, NEW YORK

DOG COLLAR CRIME

A Berkley Prime Crime Book / published by arrangement with the author

PRINTING HISTORY
Diamond edition / May 1993
Berkley Prime Crime edition / August 1994

All rights reserved.
Copyright © 1993 by Charter Communications, Inc.
This book may not be reproduced in whole or in part,
by mimeograph or any other means, without permission.
For information address: The Berkley Publishing Group,
200 Madison Avenue, New York, NY 10016.

ISBN: 0-425-14857-2

Berkley Prime Crime Books are published
by The Berkley Publishing Group,
200 Madison Avenue, New York, NY 10016.
The name BERKLEY PRIME CRIME and the
BERKLEY PRIME CRIME
design are trademarks belonging to Berkley Publishing Corporation.

PRINTED IN THE UNITED STATES OF AMERICA

10 9 8 7 6 5 4 3 2

DOG COLLAR CRIME

CHAPTER 1

Among the members of the executive committee of the Greater Palmer Dog Fanciers Association, all was not well. Angry retorts flew fast and furious between the former friends who made up the small group. Committee meetings were often contentious affairs, and when the object of the committee's interest was a subject close to everyone's heart—as it was among the Palmer Dog Fanciers—feelings were often hurt. The monthly committee meetings had never been particularly pleasurable.

But no other meeting had approached this March debacle for sheer venom. In all the thirteen years that the executive committee had assembled, never had the members of the small group exhibited such animosity toward one another.

A stout woman of a certain age was speaking in a low, throaty voice that was accustomed to command. Her figure amply filled the large armchair from which, for the last half hour, she had been launching rockets of recrimination and missiles of disgust.

"You did it *deliberately,* Melvin. Don't try to hide it. You played a dirty trick on me, to humiliate me and embarrass me."

"Thalia, for the last time, just shut your trap." The man

1

accused of playing a dirty trick was standing near a portable bar in the corner. From a ceramic pitcher in the shape of a basset hound, he added a touch of water to a stiff Scotch on the rocks. His name was Melvin Sweeten, and he was widely known to breed the finest championship basset hounds in the country. He was also the owner of Mel Sweeten's Dog Academy, a training school and kennel that he operated here on his own property. He had made quite a lot of money off of other people's dogs, but his heart belonged to bassets.

The decor of his living room was a testament to his devotion to the breed: the room was lit by basset-hound lamps and decorated with portraits of bassets. On the tables were ashtrays and coasters that had been painted with the likenesses of bassets, and before the fireplace was a large ottoman whose needlepointed cover showed a basset curled up, asleep.

Mel Sweeten bore a certain resemblance to a basset hound himself: his ears had long, dangling lobes covered with a fine peach fuzz, and his lower eyelids seemed to droop in the middle. His belly protruded, and his legs were a bit too short for his torso. His feet were enormous and rather thick. Most of the time his face had a worried look. He looked even more worried than usual tonight.

He wheeled on Thalia Gilmore, the stout woman who had accused him. "I'm sick and tired of listening to you nag. Just give it up. There is absolutely nothing wrong with the hound you bought from me. There is everything wrong with the way you have handled him, from the beginning. You totally ruined him for anything serious, and he was the best pup in the litter."

"Pah!" spat Thalia Gilmore. "Best pup you could find at the Humane Society, you mean."

Mel Sweeten shook his head. He and Thalia Gilmore had been having this argument for nearly two years now. Somehow she always managed to bring the subject up. She had bought a puppy from Sweeten, one of a litter born to Ch. Nightingale of the Forest, otherwise known as Karen. Karen was now snoozing outside in her kennel with her friend and sometime consort, Ch. Dartagnan's Finest Hour, known familiarly as Fred.

Karen had been carefully bred three or four times, and her pups had always met with great success—all but the one that had been sold to Thalia Gilmore, which had somehow turned out badly. Thalia Gilmore claimed that Mel had swindled her, substituting a dog-pound refugee for a champion pup. Sweeten claimed that Thalia Gilmore had ruined the dog by not knowing how to handle him properly. It was the old Nature *versus* Nurture controversy, in microcosm.

"I warned you that bassets are difficult. They are not a breed for amateurs," Sweeten said condescendingly.

"Did you hear that, Dick?" bellowed Thalia Gilmore. She was appealing to the third member of the executive committee, Dick Buzone, a lanky, red-haired man of middle age who was lounging on the sofa. His pale skin seemed to shine in the light cast by the basset-hound lamp at his elbow, and his yellowish eyes glittered strangely. He had heard this argument many, many times.

"Both of you are just tiresome," he said in his reedy voice. "Just forget it, Thalia. Move on."

"Move on? Did you hear that insult? How dare he call me an amateur?" By now the stout woman was quivering with rage.

"Probably no worse than a lot of other things one might say about you, Thalia," said Mel Sweeten. He took a stiff swallow of Scotch.

"You *humiliated* me, in front of all my friends, with your

dirty trick. Trying to pass that mongrel off as a purebred dog. You will pay for humiliating me, Melvin. And you will pay for what you did to poor Clematis in Philadelphia."

"Oh, lay off, Thalia. I never touched Clematis. She was sick from the chicken livers you fed her the night before. You should know better than that."

"We have a lot to talk about tonight," Buzone reminded them, glancing at his watch, "and I have to leave in half an hour. So I suggest you stop your childish squabbling and let us get on with the business at hand. Mel, you've had enough to drink. You always get nasty when you drink, and you've heaped more than enough abuse on Thalia. So knock it off. Let's get to work."

Buzone reached for a clipboard on the coffee table and harangued them with the points that needed to be covered. The first big dog show of the spring season was right around the corner, and as judges and organizers of the event they had a great many important tasks yet to perform—setting up the ticket booth, designating volunteers to the clean-up crew, and, most important of all, discussing the sponsorship of the Palmer Dog Fanciers cup. There were two dog-food companies in hot competition for the honor, but Buzone was in favor of giving the sponsorship this year to a pharmaceutical company that had developed a new heartworm pill. He didn't mention to the other two members of the committee that he had just bought a large block of shares in the drug company, but pushed for his position on other grounds.

The argument had gone on for a good twenty-five minutes when a baying noise erupted outside. Something or someone had aroused Fred and Karen from their slumber. Stiffly, Sweeten got up to find out what had caused the disturbance, leaving Thalia Gilmore alone with Dick Buzone. She instantly turned on him.

"If you don't back me up on this, Dick, I might have to go to Am-DOG and tell them what I know."

Am-DOG was the American Dog Owners Group, the watchdog organization that established all the guidelines for breeders, show judges, and competitors in the dog-show circuit. Dick Buzone was president of the Palmer chapter of Am-DOG, but he was known to be in bad standing with the national president, who wanted him out. Nobody was certain about the reasons for the animosity between the two, but it was widely known to exist.

"Shut up, Thalia," said Buzone mildly. "You talk too much."

"He poisoned Clematis in Philadelphia. You know it as well as I do. He put something in her carry crate."

"Thalia, that's water over the dam. That was seven months ago."

"Seven months. That's right. Perhaps I should charge you interest on the two thousand dollars you owe me."

"I don't owe you a nickel, Thalia."

"You *promised* me, absolutely promised. And first Clematis was poisoned by that man, and then he sold me a dog with forged papers."

"I never promised you anything, Thalia." He turned on her. "And I suggest that if you want to play with the big boys in this game, you learn to keep your mouth shut."

She appeared to digest this advice, which had sounded more like a threat than anything Buzone had uttered so far. The two sat a few moments longer in uneasy silence. Finally, Sweeten came back in the room.

Fred and Karen had stopped their baying, but Sweeten looked shaken and pale.

"Got a prowler?" Buzone asked, his tone bored.

"Something like that," replied Sweeten.

The three uneasy allies went on with their meeting.

In another fifteen minutes Buzone had prevailed, the heartworm-pill company had been awarded the sponsorship, and the meeting broke up on a note of boredom, with enmity all around.

CHAPTER 2

"Oh, yeah? Well, *I* heard your dog was afraid," said Eric Persil contentiously. "I heard that when it happened, he just ran away and left his owner there to die, because he was a *coward*."

Peter Walsh didn't bother to respond to the insult. He merely reached over and scratched Jake behind the left ear. Jake stirred but did not open his eyes. Apparently he would ignore the affront too.

Peter's friend Isaac Cook, however, was not one to take such matters lightly. Besides, he had himself once been skeptical of Jake, but Isaac had learned to admire and respect him. As Isaac's practiced fingers flew skillfully over the buttons controlling the Nintendo game, he pried his glance away from the television screen for an instant— just long enough to give Eric Persil a withering look.

Ordinarily, that look of Isaac's was enough to send his classmates running for cover. But it didn't seem to be working on this cold and rainy March afternoon.

"Well, look at him," persisted Eric defiantly. "He just *sleeps* all day."

"I wouldn't be too sure about it, Eric," replied Peter. "Could be that Jake's just resting up so he can take a bite out of you later."

7

Some people.

While speculation about his mettle raged around him, Jake was drowsily dreaming on the floor, stretched out lengthwise with his back along the length of the sofa in Peter's den. Peter was seated on the floor next to him, also with his back against the sofa. He ran his fingers up through the long, thick fur on the back of Jake's broad shoulders. Jake moved his left front paw in sleepy response, resting it on Peter's outstretched leg.

Jake was a German shepherd—or, if you took Isaac Cook as your authority, an Alsatian shepherd—a veteran of impressive years, with an interesting but incomplete personal history. He had turned up one morning on Peter's doorstep with a bullet wound in one leg and in need of a friend.

That was some months ago. Since the day of his arrival, the dog, whom Peter had christened Jake, had shown no interest in wandering off again. A dog in need of a home is clever indeed if he manages to find a boy in need of a dog.

Jake's cleverness was not under discussion, however; it was his reputation for courage that Eric Persil was determined to savage.

"He doesn't look very brave to me."

Isaac glowered. "You don't know anything, Eric, so why don't you just shut up?"

Peter thumbed through a pile of old comic books on the floor, selected one, and began to read. Peter's collection of old Superman and Spiderman adventures was legendary— the comic books had belonged to his mother when she was a little girl. Nobody was allowed to touch them but Peter and Isaac—so having them out today was kind of rubbing Eric's nose in it.

Eric Persil had never been one to take a hint, however. He had been there for four hours, and showed no interest in leaving until he had got some information. Like everyone else in the fifth-grade class, he was intensely curious about Peter's dog. He had heard rumors.

For starters, Eric had heard that Peter's dog had once belonged to an ex-cop named Matt Dugan. He had also heard that Dugan had been murdered in the seediest neighborhood in Palmer, right behind a nightclub called Leanna's Piano Parlor, and that the dog had been there. Now Eric was trying to pry some inside facts out of Peter.

He had tried the direct approach earlier in the afternoon, but he had been swiftly rebuffed. Now, in his frustrated desire to force from Peter the particulars about Jake, he had resorted to casting aspersions on Jake's character. Even Eric Persil, clumsy and bullying as he was, should have known that this was the wrong procedure.

Peter and Isaac, when they discovered that Jake had once belonged to a murder victim, had embarked on a clandestine bus ride across town one day to take a chilling look at the scene of the crime. There had still been faint chalk marks on the asphalt, indicating the spot where Dugan had fallen, and ominous-looking dark stains that could *easily* have been bloodstains. Probably were bloodstains, the boys had later concurred.

This was the sort of information that Peter and Isaac would never grant to Eric Persil, whom they tolerated but did not actually like. Eric was at Peter's house today through one of those arrangements that mothers make for everyone to have fun together. Peter and Isaac, by tacit consent, were being polite without giving an inch. Eric, they agreed, was sort of a pain. There had been no need to discuss tactics.

"Well?" Eric persisted. "If he's such a great dog, how come the guy that owned him is dead?"

Peter replied without raising his eyes from the page. "Because he was murdered," he said in a reasonable voice.

He might have been discussing fractions or geography, for all the interest that he permitted himself to show. Peter liked to keep things to himself.

"Yeah," agreed Isaac, with passion. "And you'd be dead too if somebody pulled a Magnum on you." He made a pistol with his right hand, aimed at Eric, and fired, making a noise like a gun. Then he turned his attention back to the game in progress, Super Mario Brothers.

"Unh-unh," protested Eric. "Not if I had a really *good* guard dog. A *really* good one, not some dog that the police didn't want anymore."

"Shut up, Eric," said Isaac again, his eyes glued to the television screen.

From Peter's and Isaac's point of view, the subject of Jake's bravery wasn't even debatable; still, it was a fascinating subject, one that merited constant discussions between the two friends, and other people as well.

"So?" Eric's voice had become a whine. "Why didn't he attack the guy?"

"Look. Maybe he did," said Peter. "We weren't there, so how do we know? Maybe he bit the guy. Took off his right arm, all the way up to the elbow."

"He looks too old."

In truth Jake did look as though he might be past his prime. His brown and black coat was tinged with gray, and there were a few pale whitish hairs around his muzzle. But Peter and Isaac knew that Jake could be ferocious— they had put him through his paces one day, and had been amazed at the results. That had been just shortly after they learned that Jake had once been a member of the Palmer K-9 squad. Retired, with distinction, Peter had later been told. Upon his retirement from the K-9 squad, Jake had gone to live with Matt Dugan—who was also retired from the Palmer police, but not with distinction.

"Jake's not too old," Peter replied. He carefully turned the page of the Superman adventure. The story involved Mr. Mxylptlx, one of Peter's favorite villains.

Eric persisted, switching to a logical approach. He leaned forward earnestly.

"Look—if he *bit* the guy, then the police should be able to find him. Like at the hospital, getting his arm sewed back on or something. But my dad told me that they never caught the guy. So your dog *didn't* bite him. He just ran away, probably because he's too old."

"He's not too old," Peter repeated in a tone of certainty. Jake's bullet wound had been proof enough, for Peter, that the dog had fought bravely. But he didn't go into it with Eric. What was more, Jake had recently been called upon to use his skills right here in Peter's own house—he had saved Peter's mother from the frenzied attack of an intruder. Inevitably, this tale too had gotten around a little bit, but Peter didn't like to talk about it. That had been serious stuff, and Peter had been frightened. Of course, Isaac knew the whole story, but Isaac and Peter weren't about to let a nerd like Eric in on the details.

"You don't know if Jake even defended the guy," said Eric. "You weren't even there."

Isaac, nearing the end of his Nintendo game, was also reaching the limit of his patience. He turned to stare at Eric. "Listen," he commanded, pointing an imperious finger at Eric Persil. "What the police know and don't know, *maybe* we know and maybe we don't. But if you don't shut up we'll sic Jake on you, and he'll rip you to shreds. And then we'll go and scatter the pieces out in the country, and nobody will ever know what happened to you."

"Hey, Isaac, is that a promise or a threat?" Eric did his best to sound sarcastic. "I don't believe this old mutt's got what it takes." He glanced nervously toward the sleeping dog. He didn't sound convinced. "Gimme that." He grabbed the Nintendo controls from Isaac.

Peter and Isaac exchanged a look. Eric Persil was a colossal pain.

Peter sighed and turned a page of the comic book. "Hey, Eric. What time is your mother coming to pick you up?"

Not far away from Peter Walsh's house, at the Central Precinct of the Palmer police department, Jake was a subject of another, equally considered debate.

Cosmo Gordon was easing his large frame back into the well-worn wooden armchair opposite Lieutenant Michael McGowan's desk. Gordon dropped a manila envelope on the floor. The envelope landed with a loud slap. In it was a postmortem report for McGowan. "So, Mike, what's eating you?"

"Hi, Cosmo." He was leaning comfortably back in his swivel chair, his long fingers toying idly with a rubber band. He looked relaxed; but Cosmo Gordon, who knew him well, could sense the worry. The senior medical examiner in Palmer, Gordon had worked with McGowan on hundreds of homicides, and the two were close friends despite the twenty-year difference in their ages. "Brought the report?" asked McGowan.

Gordon nodded.

McGowan, his dark blue eyes in shadow, scowled up at the medical examiner. "Cosmo, I've been thinking about it, and I have to tell you I'm still kind of worried. I'm not sure it's safe for her to keep that animal."

Gordon knew instantly who the "her" was—Jackie Walsh, the woman who, with her young son, had adopted Matt Dugan's dog. The dog had been present at the time of Dugan's murder, and there had been some talk in police circles that the animal might be useful, when and if the murderer was caught.

"We've been over all this, Mike," answered Gordon. "She didn't seem to me to be likely to change her mind about it. They're both too attached, both she and the boy. Besides, she's probably better off with a guard dog."

Gordon had remarked to his wife Nancy, just the other day, that McGowan had obviously fallen for Jackie Walsh.

Gordon didn't blame the younger man. Jackie Walsh was a very attractive woman, with energy and brains to match. An instructor in the film department at Rodgers University, she had recently been involved in a homicide case. Involved, hell, thought Gordon. She had helped them nail the murderer, and without her the Palmer police would have been nowhere on the case. A spunky woman.

But she was also recently divorced, and gave every indication of wanting to keep her distance—not just from McGowan, it was nothing personal—from men in general. In Gordon's book, being gun-shy was understandable—but it looked like McGowan was declining to understand.

"A watchdog, sure," said McGowan, opening a palm, conceding a point. "But Dugan's dog? That animal's not a pet, it's a police dog. Not a family friend."

"You forget that Dugan and the dog retired at about the same time," said Gordon. "The dog's had four or five years to adapt to retirement. Besides, if anyone is a friend to that family, it's the dog. Don't forget what happened to Philip Barger's murderer, right there in Jackie Walsh's kitchen."

"Yeah." McGowan considered it. The dog had saved Jackie's life. "I wish we could get the guy who killed Dugan, though. I'd feel better about the whole thing."

"Well, now you're talking. That's what you should really be worrying about, Mike. Not about Jackie. Any leads?"

"No." McGowan shook his head. "It's been more than two months now, and the trail's pretty cold."

"What about the weapon?"

"It hasn't turned up yet—but you know the way with that kind of thing. Either the gun got tossed somewhere, and it'll turn up eventually, or the guy's still got it, and he'll use it again, and then it will still turn up eventually. Ballistics has the info, and when that gun shows we'll get the shooter. It's a waiting game."

"I wish I had paid closer attention to him that night," said Gordon, for perhaps the hundredth time. Shortly before his murder, Dugan had visited Gordon, an old friend from his days on the force. Since his dismissal from the Palmer police, Dugan had gone sadly downhill, drinking heavily and gambling more heavily. There had been talk that some of his bets had been bankrolled by dangerous sources, the kind of people it wasn't smart to borrow from. He had been sensitive enough about people not to ask much of his old friends, especially his cop buddies—nor had most of them sought him out. Gordon, however, had made sure to stay in touch, albeit erratically. He and Matt had been close friends, once.

The night of his visit to Gordon, Matt Dugan had talked, not very coherently, about some kind of conspiracy of corruption in the upper echelons of Palmer politics. He had also mentioned his fear that someone was out to get him.

For once, that night, Cosmo Gordon's judgment had been clouded—not by recalcitrance so much as by pity. Full of sorrow for his old friend's trembling hands and hesitant manner, Gordon hadn't really paid much attention to Dugan's ramblings. He had dismissed them as the talk of a man done in by his own weaknesses.

Three days later Dugan had been shot.

"You're right, Cosmo," said McGowan, breaking a long silence. "I have to get the shooter. Then nobody'll come after Jackie's dog."

"Mike, the dog is okay. Nobody's going to come after him. And whatever you do, skip the advice-giving. Don't try to tell her what to do—you'll only give her a reason to tell you to get lost."

"Yeah." He shot the rubber band across the room and leaned forward. "So. Speaking of dogs, I think I can guess what you've brought me. You've got the results of the postmortem on that dog man that turned up dead today. Melvin Sweeten."

CHAPTER 3

Cosmo Gordon leaned down and picked up the manila envelope from the floor, and tossed it onto McGowan's desk. In it were the contents of his postmortem examination of Melvin Sweeten, Palmer's leading dog trainer and breeder.

"Cause of death, like you thought. And the choke collar looks like it."

"Hmm," said McGowan, pulling out a sheaf of papers. He skimmed it quickly.

Most of the information merely corroborated the conclusions he had reached yesterday, when he had been summoned to examine the body of Mel Sweeten. Sweeten was fairly well known in Palmer as a dog trainer, and he ran the best boarding kennel in the city (charging correspondingly high prices). Sweeten's passion for basset hounds was also well known among those who cared about such things. Mel Sweeten's basset puppies sold for large sums, and when they grew old enough to keep from stepping on their own ears they were entered in dog shows, where they won plenty of ribbons, just for being themselves.

On Wednesday, March 23, Mel Sweeten's body had been found inside one of the dog runs at his establishment. There was a choke collar about his neck—the type used in training dogs to sit and heel. So far, the police had no leads, although the widow, naturally, was being carefully looked over as the suspect of choice.

McGowan put the report down. "And?"

"And nothing. Well, you can read it for yourself, I don't need to spoon-feed you. Time of death, between nine and midnight, give or take the usual. Don't even know why we bother with the time of death in these cases—we almost always have to include a fudge factor of an hour or so. Cause of death, asphyxiation of the glottal apparatus— oh, hell. He was strangled, Mike. Or maybe we should say choked."

"Tell me, Cosmo," said McGowan, leaning back in his chair to shoot a rubber band up at the ceiling, "what kind of guy just sits there while a murderer slips a dog collar around his neck?"

"Kinky, maybe."

"Maybe, but that's not what I've got from witnesses."

"What did they give you?"

McGowan picked up a small notebook and leaned back in his chair. He flipped through the pages, looking down now and then while he gave Gordon the known facts about Sweeten.

"Thirty-nine, married, no kids. Wife is much younger, twenty-six, called Amy. She's a researcher in the art history department at Rodgers. He was kind of a dull guy, if you ask me. Totally into his dogs, his basset hounds—but he made a nice living running a boarding school for dogs, with a staff of one. Charged top dollar."

"What did you make on the wife?"

"I talked to her yesterday afternoon. She was visiting her sister in Wardville, she says, and came home yesterday morning, just in time to find his body. We're waiting for corroboration from the sister—but why would she lie when we can easily check?"

"Huh," agreed Gordon. He stretched out his legs and contemplated his feet.

"Her late husband was widely regarded as the owner of the best strain of bassets in the country. She likes dogs all right, but she's not a fanatic. She says she isn't especially fond of basset hounds"—he consulted his notebook—"because they're 'fussy and stubborn.' Doesn't know who would want to murder him or why, thinks it must have been an accident." McGowan raised his brows. "She actually said that."

"An accident. He accidentally slipped a choke collar around his neck? And then gave it a yank?"

McGowan shrugged. "Who knows? I think she's lying, but I have Felix Cruz checking her whereabouts. Until he pokes a hole in her alibi, that's all we have."

"What time did she get in from her sister's place?"

McGowan looked at his notes. "Early. Nine-thirty, give or take. She unpacked, fixed herself a cup of coffee, and read the newspaper."

"The newspaper is delivered?"

McGowan nodded. "She says she thought that was odd, that Mel hadn't taken in the paper, or that he'd gone out before it came, she wasn't sure which."

"And then what?"

"Then she went into this little study, where she does a lot of reading, and typed up some notes she'd made at the museum in Wardville. Finally at about eleven o'clock she thought the dogs were barking too loud, or something, so she got exasperated and went out to look at them to tell them to shut up."

"Hush Puppies."

"Huh?"

"That's what those dogs are, those basset hounds. They're the Hush Puppies dogs."

"Oh." McGowan laughed. "So they are. Right. So Amy Sweeten goes out to the kennels, which are about a hundred yards from the house, to tell the puppies to hush, but before she actually gets there she sees her husband lying facedown in one of the dog runs. So she turns around and runs inside to the phone to call the doctor."

"She knew he was dead?"

"She thought he'd had a heart attack or something. But, get this, she says she didn't get close enough to him to find out whether or not he was dead." He turned a page of his notebook. "She says, 'I thought it would be more useful to solicit professional help.' " McGowan raised a brow again. "Then she waited inside for the doctor, and when he came they went to the kennel together."

Gordon was frowning. "You think?"

McGowan shrugged. "Yeah—I see it. The problem is, we've got to make it stick."

"Wife comes home from a trip and finds her husband prostrate. She doesn't bother to check if he's breathing, she just calls the old GP up the hill."

"I agree."

"Well, there's your answer. How'd she get the collar on him, though? Some kinky stuff, maybe?"

"You think?"

"Could be." Cosmo Gordon rose to leave.

"Thanks, Cosmo," said McGowan, tapping the report.

"Sure. Keep me posted. Sounds kind of interesting."

"It will be." McGowan permitted himself a smile. "I'm going to talk to all my sources at Rodgers. See what I can dig up about Amy Sweeten from her fellow faculty members."

"Uh-oh," said Gordon. The fellow faculty member in question was Jackie Walsh, of course. "You'd better handle her carefully, Mike. And for God's sake don't try to tell her how to run her life. She probably ran away from her husband because he got too bossy."

"Right," said McGowan. "I'll remember that. Thanks for telling me how to run my life. Now you run away."

Gordon left and McGowan reached for the phone. He didn't need to look up Jackie Walsh's telephone number. Inside of a minute, he had secured himself an invitation to dine tonight with Jackie and Peter. Meat loaf at seven. He smiled and hung up the phone.

CHAPTER 4

At seven thirty-five, when Michael McGowan still hadn't arrived at her newly renovated loft on Isabella Lane, Jackie Walsh found herself torn between irritation and relief.

On the one hand, McGowan had invited himself—and by this time, Peter was getting hungry and was ready for dinner. He was cranky too—probably because he'd spent a long, rainy afternoon inside with that tiresome boy, Eric Persil. Jackie told herself that she just had to learn to say no to Rosemary Persil, the boy's mother. She liked Rosemary well enough, but her son was a nuisance—a "dweeb," according to Peter and his friend Isaac. It wasn't fair to inflict the dweeb on them.

What was more, if Peter were to eat now, then it would just be Jackie and Michael having supper together later on, which was strictly not what Jackie had in mind when McGowan called. Irritating—especially since both Jackie and Peter were looking forward to seeing him. It had been several months since they'd last seen him. Jackie kind of missed him.

On the other hand, Michael's being half an hour late—more, really—meant that maybe the pressure was off. You couldn't be thirty-five minutes late—no, forty minutes late (she glanced again at her watch to make sure)—if you were trying to impress someone. Since he hadn't managed to get there on time, or even close to it, there would be no question of the lieutenant's staying too late, or wanting anything from her but information about Amy Sweeten.

That was where the relief came in, or so Jackie told herself.

Michael McGowan hadn't said so, but of course Amy Sweeten was the reason that he had called. That was fine with Jackie. The murder of Amy's husband was front-page news in Palmer, and it had caused quite a stir at Rodgers University, where Amy was well regarded by the faculty. She wasn't one of them, exactly, being only a teaching assistant and researcher; Jackie suspected that if ever Amy tried to pass herself off as being right up there with the art-history bigwigs, her colleagues would give her the cold shoulder pretty fast.

But where the outside world met the university, in that small union of the two disparate universes, it was clear who was in and who was out. In the faculty cafeteria today, at lunchtime, there had been a lot of discussion about what should and shouldn't be said by the faculty, with a great deal of accompanying talk about solidarity.

Jackie Walsh thought all of that had been nothing but claptrap and posturing. As far as she was concerned, if it was murder, then the police could have everything and welcome to it. She wasn't romantic about murderers.

Besides, Jackie liked Michael McGowan, and wouldn't have thought twice about telling him anything and everything she knew to help him with one of his cases. Last fall, when one of Jackie's colleagues in the film department had died a sudden, violent death, Jackie had found herself not only in the midst of the police investigation, but also in the thick of the university's official response to the murder. Jackie hadn't enjoyed all the politicking, but she had enjoyed—well, not *enjoyed,* but found stimulating— her involvement in catching the criminal.

Those events had struck frighteningly close to home, but over time, the memory of that fear had diminished. She had to admit to herself that she wouldn't mind being in on another murder investigation with Michael McGowan.

How far she had come in the past months! Jackie and Peter had moved to Palmer fairly recently—on the heels of Jackie's divorce from Cooper Walsh, her husband of over a decade—and Jackie had gone back to work at her old job, as an instructor in the film department at Rodgers University. She found it invigorating, to say the least, to be once more a child of the city, after her long suburban exile in Kingswood, which was a good forty minutes from downtown. It was wonderful to be working for herself again, after all those years of dancing to Cooper's tune. Of course, there was a good reason for her harsh opinion of those days.

She didn't think of those married years as wasted, exactly; but when she fled the suburbs she had also fled, with her whole heart, the life of a suburban housewife. She just hadn't been cut out for it—she had simply been the wrong wife for Cooper. She had, unfortunately, too many ideas of her own.

Cooper thought that suburban life was perfect, and, moreover, that suburban wives should just sit back and enjoy what came their way. He had been a good provider, and had thrilled to barbecues and golf on the weekends. Jackie, on the other hand, hated golf, and wasn't even really keen on barbecues. She failed to see the romance, especially since Cooper had insisted on buying one of those fancy propane grills. The propane had killed Jackie's enthusiasm for barbecues altogether.

Yet she had been content to follow Cooper's lead, to answer his needs. She had considered that her part of the bargain; after all, he devoted himself to providing for them, right? So she had spent the prime of her life taking his shirts to the laundry, picking up his socks off the floor, cooking his favorite meals, and rearing their child. All of which might have been fine—but Cooper had repaid Jackie's devotion by falling in love with someone else. So Jackie had promptly decamped, taking Peter with her. She had no regrets, and surprisingly little bitterness. Nor would she ever go back.

It had been less than a year since her return to Palmer, but already Jackie felt whole again. She had worried that she might be lonely, but with Peter around she never felt alone. What was more, the job of renovating and decorating their loft on Isabella Lane had filled many of her long evenings at first; and of course as a Palmer native Jackie had ties to the place. Her mother lived only about twenty minutes away, and there were still a few friends from high school around. Even an old boyfriend or two—but from them Jackie kept her distance. She wanted no part of romantic entanglements.

On the other hand, there was Michael McGowan, who was certainly an interesting specimen.

When McGowan finally showed, at a quarter to eight, Jackie had forgotten her irritation with him for being late. It was good to see him again, and Peter was delighted; even Jake seemed to remember him, greeting him with a welcoming bark and a vigorous session of tail-wagging. McGowan quickly enlivened their little dinner circle with hilarious stories about the fat, slow-witted sergeant in Missing Persons, who was known as the Meatball. Jackie was soon very glad McGowan had come.

When dinner was over, and Peter had sped away to his

room to finish up his homework, McGowan rose and began to help out with the dishes.

"Sorry I was so late," he said, pouring soap into the sink. He grinned at Jackie.

"It's all right," she answered. "I suppose you want to ask me about Amy Sweeten."

"Is it that obvious?"

"Well—of course. And why not?" Jackie brushed back a curl of her lustrous dark hair and smiled at him. "It's not as though her husband's murder isn't all over the news. And art historians *do* sometimes get to know film instructors." She filled two mugs full of steaming hot coffee for them, brought a plate of homemade ginger cookies to the kitchen table, and sat. "Forget the dishes. Come and have some coffee and ginger cookies. Then you can go ahead and grill me."

"All right." McGowan dried his hands and joined Jackie at the table. He reached for his coffee mug. "Tell me what you know about her."

"Not much, really—but I hated to disappoint you, so I've been thinking long and hard about her all afternoon. I've met her, of course, and seen her at various functions around school—meetings, faculty teas, that sort of thing. Socially our paths don't really cross all that often, but she was at a baby shower I went to about ten days ago. For one of the members of the English department."

"And?"

Jackie leaned back in her chair and crossed her arms. "Off the record, of course."

"Of course. This is unofficial. If anyone wants to know why I came here tonight, you can tell them it was just for the pleasure of your company. Yours and Peter's."

"And Jake's."

"Of course. I thought that went without saying."

"Okay. My impression of her—have you seen her?"

"You bet. I spent most of yesterday afternoon with her."

"Then you know what she looks like—really pale, really thin, with that pale golden hair. Not naturally thin, but as though she doesn't eat right."

"I'd agree with that. Although I wasn't sure if it was just the shock of her husband's death."

"No." Jackie shook her head. "It may be more noticeable now, but that's the way she generally looks." McGowan waited patiently, his blue eyes sparkling. Finally Jackie went on. "Rodgers is a pretty big place, but you get to hear things about people. I've heard that Amy Sweeten is a little bit strange."

"Why?"

Jackie shrugged her shoulders. "That I can't tell you. But she always seems kind of preoccupied, and unhappy, with that pale face that never sees the sun."

"So you saw her at this party. Did she have fun there, at least?"

"No. She was absolutely miserable, and paler than usual. Much paler."

"Why?"

"Well, I did try to guess, that night, but I sort of figured it was for the obvious reason—the subject, babies. She doesn't have a baby, no children. And I know that to be at a party like that, if you don't have a baby and desperately want one, can be really tough. Wishing the new mother well, and wanting so much to be a mother yourself."

McGowan eyed Jackie thoughtfully. Peter was ten years old; he had put Jackie, at a guess, somewhere between thirty-six and thirty-nine. So perhaps there had been a time when she had wanted a baby, like that.

Jackie knew what McGowan was thinking, and she

ignored him. Her comment had invited speculation, but she hoped he would keep his distance. "I sat next to her the whole night, and I had the impression that there were difficulties."

"Marital difficulties, or physical?"

"I couldn't tell you for sure, but here's something you should know. Just a general fact. When women get together for an occasion like that, they tend to be rather free with information about their physical states. I prefer not to join in, and frankly I hate it when a roomful of women who are comparative strangers to each other just go ahead and spill the beans about how hard *they* had to try to get pregnant, or they compare the embarrassing personal medical details about their deliveries. They like to talk about centimeters, and that kind of thing."

"Not your bag," affirmed McGowan. He looked gratified. He wasn't sure what the centimeters were all about, but he was pretty sure he didn't want to know.

"Right. Not my bag. But there's something about the chemistry at a baby shower that makes people spill that sort of thing. It's like an encounter group, or group therapy, with gifts. God, how I hate showers."

"Me too."

Jackie flashed him a smile. "Well, Amy Sweeten just sat there on the sofa all night and hardly said a word. She wouldn't touch the food, which was terrific, and she wouldn't drink anything but tap water with a little slice of lemon in it. She just sat there, listening to everyone's stories and, it seemed to me, trying not to cry. She left as soon as she could. So that was how I got the impression that she was upset by the occasion."

"Hmm."

"I know—it's not much. But I thought maybe it was a sign of some kind of trouble, one way or another."

"What's the dope on her at Rodgers? Is she well thought of?"

Jackie nodded. "She has a reputation for being a real workhorse. Long, long hours, assembling the slides for all the art-history lectures, taking photographs of paintings and developing them, getting down details for the professors, who are either too busy or too lazy to do the work for themselves. The joke that goes around is that they hope she'll never finish her dissertation. They need her too much."

"Right." He reached for a cookie. "Did you make these?"

"Of course."

"Not 'of course.' Plenty of very accomplished people can't make ginger cookies. I'm glad you can. Now, what about her husband?"

"Don't know. I never met him—he didn't come to the baby shower."

"No, I guess not." McGowan reached for his coffee cup and sipped at it thoughtfully. "It's kind of strange, don't you think, that a woman with her nose in the library would marry a man whose interests are all outdoorsy? A dog trainer."

"Maybe, maybe not."

McGowan sighed and asked Jackie a few more routine questions about her colleague. There really wasn't much more Jackie could offer, but she promised McGowan that she would keep her eyes and ears open. He told her—in the strictest confidence, and totally unofficially—about some of the information in the postmortem report, and about Amy's discovery of the body as she had related it. These details weren't exactly secrets, but they weren't going to be given to just anyone.

Jackie agreed with McGowan—it was extremely odd that

Amy had called the doctor before checking to see if Mel was all right. But, then again, Amy was sort of a matter-of-fact person. Either she had behaved very sensibly, or she had been suffering from shock.

Peter, finished with his homework, came downstairs to say good night. Jackie went up with him—*not,* as they told McGowan plainly, to tuck him in or anything, but just to be sure he turned off his light.

When she returned to the kitchen McGowan had finished the dishes.

What a man, thought Jackie, although she didn't say it aloud. It could be that he was only trying to impress her, and that the dish-doing wasn't part of his regular repertoire. There were men who had been known to put on saintlike performances in that area, only to reveal their true natures later on.

But in spite of herself Jackie was sufficiently impressed to allow the conversation to shift to more general things; and it was nearly midnight before McGowan, looking very pleased with himself, headed home.

Jackie Walsh, as she bade good night to Jake and head-ed upstairs to bed, was full of curiosity. McGowan had given her some of the details of Mel Sweeten's death—which had been fairly grisly. Just on the face of it Jackie doubted that Amy would have the strength to strangle a man to death, even with a choke collar. And then there was the question of their relative heights. McGowan told Jackie that Mel Sweeten had been about six feet tall. Amy was a little thing—probably at least nine inches shorter, and weighing about a hundred ten pounds. To Jackie's knowledge, Amy had never been seen at any of the faculty aerobics classes, or playing squash at the gym. She wasn't the athletic type.

. As Jackie dropped off to sleep, she tried to imagine it, and couldn't. Dimly she wondered if perhaps Amy had stood on a milking stool or a crate or something to yank the choke collar tight. Otherwise, she'd never have gotten the leverage she needed to kill her husband.

CHAPTER 5

Jackie Walsh wasn't really sure why she did what she did on the Saturday following Michael McGowan's visit. In the days to come she would wonder about it again and again, speculating that she might be growing nosy, or obsessed with murder, or maybe just losing her marbles.

But on that Saturday morning, with Peter out of town visiting his father, and with no real program in mind, she took Jake over to Mel Sweeten's Dog Academy to sign him up for a refresher course in obedience training.

Not that Jake needed training—he was far and away the most obedient dog that Jackie had ever known. He seemed to be able to tell by the look on your face what you wanted him to do next; and he responded to oral commands with an alacrity that belied his years. So as they drove the two miles to the Dog Academy, which was on the far side of the university, near the Palmer city limits, Jackie offered Jake a brief apology.

"I hope you won't feel like a pawn," she said to him.

Jake, in the backseat, drooped his head over and rested his chin on Jackie's right shoulder.

"Or a toy, a trifle, a cat's paw," she went on.

Jake let out a low growl.

"It's just that you're the best excuse in the world to go out there. So I will *have* to use you." She reached her hand back and scratched Jake gently on the furry middle part of his nose. "I hope you won't feel it's all too undignified to be borne."

Jake emitted a low *woof,* and he and Jackie drove the rest of the way in silence.

She had supposed that other people besides herself would be curious about the scene of the crime. She thought that all the dog owners in Palmer would turn up, asking for boarding room for the night for Fido. Jackie thought she might have to stand in line, buy a ticket to look at the sights—*step right up!* But as she pulled her gray-and-red Jeep into the parking lot, she noted that there was only one other car there.

She and Jake climbed out and presented themselves at a small, ramshackle clapboard shed, with a sign saying OFFICE over the door. She and Jake stepped in out of the freezing cold March air, drawing only vague looks from the three other people present.

A large, red-faced man with fat, freckled arms and beefy fists sat behind a desk; a little plastic plaque riding in a brass-rimmed holder identified him as Tom Mann, Manager. Jackie could tell at a glance that the two overcoated visitors on her side of the desk—big, square-jawed, square-shouldered men with closely cropped hair and well-polished, square-toed shoes—were city employees. She would have bet even money that they were undercover detectives. She would have taken odds that they worked for Michael McGowan.

Trying to look as though she never thought about anything but dogs, Jackie plopped down on a chair to wait her turn. Jake sat down quietly at her feet, lifting his chin a bit in a way that gave him an unquestionably noble aspect. Jackie noticed that he gave the detectives a tolerant, almost respectful glance. There must be something about the way they carry themselves, she reflected, or maybe there was a particular scent at the precinct house.

The detectives, for their part, had obviously not recognized Jake as one of their own. They didn't give him a second look. That was just as well, Jackie thought. It wouldn't do for Michael McGowan to hear that she'd been snooping around at the Dog Academy. Michael would know in a minute that she wasn't interested in furthering Jake's education.

Apparently the detectives were winding up their business. One of them was busily putting away his notebook, while the other dropped a card on Tom Mann's desk.

"Anything else you think of, anything at all, and you let us hear from you," he said, sliding the card toward Mann. "All right?"

"Sure thing," responded Mann, in a kind of hearty-squeaky voice that reminded Jackie of Keenan Wynn. Or maybe it was Ed Wynn. She never could remember which was which, and always had to check the film credits carefully—which was embarrassing for a film instructor, to say the least. Mann's voice had that same high, breezy quality, almost a laryngitic squeal. Jackie always distrusted people with voices like that.

Tom Mann rose from behind the desk and shook the officers' hands. "Sure thing. I'm glad you fellows are on the job. I mean to write the police commissioner and tell him so."

"No need for that," responded the talkative one. Jackie wondered if the other one ever opened his mouth. "Just doing our job," the detective added. He turned smartly on his heel and nodded to the silent partner, and the two men strode out. He ought to have touched the brim of his fedora, thought Jackie—except he wasn't wearing a fedora. The hat would have completed the impersonation of Robert Stack as Eliot Ness. Even without the hat, it wasn't a bad performance. Much as there was to admire about Kevin Costner, she really thought Robert Stack had been the perfect Ness, capturing the stern-jawed rectitude of the man week after week on the old television series.

"Help you, ma'am?" came Tom Mann's squeak.

"Oh, yes please." She rose and turned to Jake. "You *stay,* boy. *Stay,*" she said in the pleading voice of one accustomed to disobedience. The little charade wasn't fair to Jake, but he didn't look as though his feelings had been hurt. He blinked at her and stayed. Jackie went to the desk.

"My son and I have recently adopted this dog, from—from a friend," she lied, "who couldn't keep him anymore, who was, um, moving. Moving to New York. And since we've never *had* a dog before, and since he's not really *our* dog, and he's kind of old, I thought it would be a good idea to bring him by." She glanced nervously over her shoulder at Jake, who was still staying. "I would think that he could be kind of ferocious, and I want to make sure he knows that he has to do what we tell him to do. And a friend of mine mentioned that you have short courses in obedience training, so we thought—"

"Whoa, now, whoa," said Tom Mann. "First, let's have some information." He indicated the chair just in front of the desk, and Jackie obediently sat in it. Then, just as swiftly, she took a moment to marvel at her instantaneous response to his gesture. It must have something to do with all those years of teaching dogs to sit, she thought, amazed.

Tom Mann pulled out a small white file card from his

top drawer and grabbed a pen from a holder. "Name?"

"Jackie Walsh."

"No—I mean his name." Mann nodded to indicate Jake.

"Oh—he's called Jake."

"Just 'Jake'?"

"Sure. He doesn't need a last name, does he? If he needs one, he can use ours."

"No, he doesn't need one," said Mann, printing carefully. J-A-K-E. "No, he doesn't. On the other hand, he looks like a fine purebred shepherd to me, Mrs., um—"

"Walsh. Ms."

"*Miz* Walsh," said Mann, drawing the syllable out. Evidently Tom Mann, Manager, didn't approve of "Ms." "He looks like a dog with papers. And a dog that comes with papers generally comes with more than just 'Jake' for a name. You know—like a big white standard poodle might be called 'Champion Ferdinand's Boules de Neige,' on its papers, and just be called 'Frenchie' by his owner. But if its owner tells us we're training 'Boules de Neige' you can be pretty sure we'll ask the owner a question or two about the dog's parentage, see what kind of stock he comes from, and so forth. That way, we get a deeper understanding of the individual animal."

"Oh." Jackie glanced over her shoulder at Jake, who was still staying. "Well, if he's got some kind of fancy background, we don't know anything about it."

"Uh-huh." Mann didn't look as though he believed her, for some reason. Jackie tried to look nonchalant.

"Age?" asked Tom Mann.

"Um, we're not certain. About ten, I think."

"What about your friends? Didn't the people who gave him to you know how old their own dog was?"

"I don't think so," said Jackie. "As far as I know, they got him from the pound."

"Uh-huh," said Mann, his squeak even more skeptical than before.

He got up from behind his desk and crossed to where Jake was sitting. "Good boy," he said, extending the back of his right hand for Jake to sniff.

With a glance for Jackie, Jake leaned forward and duly sniffed. He didn't look impressed, but neither was he evidently annoyed.

"Good *boy,* Jake," said Jackie in an artificially bright voice. Jake gave her a look.

Mann squatted down, duck-walked forward about a foot, and put a hand up toward Jake's mouth. Very gingerly, he lifted one of Jake's lips to take a look at the dog's teeth; then he rose to his full height.

Jake stayed.

At least six feet two, thought Jackie, studying Tom Mann. He could have done it easily, without needing to stand on a crate or anything.

"I'd say about ten is right," said Mann. He circled back to his chair behind the desk and took up his pen once more. "Okay. What you'd probably like, *Miz* Walsh, is to let us give the dog a series of basic tests to evaluate his obedience skills. When that's done, we'll enroll him at whatever level seems most appropriate. I don't imagine you want to show him?"

"You mean, in a dog show?"

"Not a horse show." Mann chuckled at his little joke.

"Well, do you know it hadn't entered my mind," said Jackie, voice full of rising interest. "I've never even been to a dog show."

"Well, showing is a lot of fun if you have the stamina and the interest, but it's not something that appeals to everyone. If you don't mind my saying so, Mrs. Walsh, you don't seem the type for it somehow."

So they were back to "Mrs." Jackie let it go—she wanted information. "Probably not," she agreed, looking thoughtful. "But tell me, Mr. Mann—"

"Call me Tom. Everyone does."

"Okay." Jackie smiled brightly. "Tell me—if I were to sign Jake up for a class here, I think I would really have to see the grounds. Could you show me around?"

"We do our obedience training right out front there." He gestured toward the large field that separated the kennel operation from the house.

"Oh." Jackie bit her lip. "But what if Jake needs to spend the night? I'll have to inspect the dogs' living quarters, I think, before—"

"Look, Mrs. Walsh. *If* that's your name." Tom Mann had risen suddenly from his chair, and he stood glowering at Jackie. He raised his voice and pointed an accusing finger at her. "I don't want to be rude, but we've had an awful lot of reporters snooping around out here. Some of them showed their credentials, nice and polite and professional. Some of them pretended they wanted to have their dogs trained. They were a *little* bit better at it than you are—because at least they brought their own dogs with them, not some rent-a-dog from the nearest kennel." He gestured sharply toward Jake.

Jake looked solemnly at Mann.

"Stay, Jake," said Jackie calmly, her voice full of authority. "Good boy. Just stay."

Mann resumed his tirade. "I think we've had enough to deal with here at the Dog Academy, without this kind of nonsense. It's rude, nosy people like you who make things like this intolerable. So I suggest that you get out, and quit wasting my time—"

He stopped abruptly and looked up toward the office door, which had suddenly opened, letting in the cold, wet

March air. Amy Sweeten stepped in quietly and closed the door behind her.

"Something wrong, Tom?" she asked.

Amy must have heard him bellowing, thought Jackie.

"No, Amy. Nothing wrong." He glared at Jackie. "Just getting rid of a snoopy reporter, that's all."

Amy Sweeten allowed her glance to fall on the client seated at the desk.

"Jackie?"

"Um, hi, Amy," Jackie replied, working hard to hide her embarrassment. "I was awfully sorry to hear about Mel. Are you all right?"

"I'm fine. Thanks." Amy Sweeten looked back at Tom. "That's not a reporter, Tom. That's Jackie Walsh. She teaches at Rodgers."

"Well, what's she doing here, Mrs. Sweeten?" asked Mann in a complaining voice. He glowered at Jake. "With that animal?"

Amy glanced at Jake. "Well, Tom, if I had to guess, I'd say that's her dog, a stray that she took in last fall. She told me all about him at a party we went to two weeks ago. His name is Jake." She transferred her glance back to Mann, who was still standing behind the desk. "Since he *was* a stray probably Jackie has come here to ask about an obedience course for him. Fix her up, please. And give her a discount. Twenty percent. She's a colleague."

"Oh, Amy, that's—" Jackie began.

Amy waved her interruption away. "Jackie, when Tom is through maybe you wouldn't mind coming up to the house for a cup of tea? You're exactly the person I wanted to see."

CHAPTER 6

It had taken Jackie less than a minute to get over her embarrassment from the encounter with Amy. For Tom Mann, Manager, it hadn't been so easy. He had begun with profuse apologies, but Jackie had waved them away. Then he had graciously proposed a tour of the Academy's grounds. This suggestion Jackie declined—she had decided, while Mann was talking, that she would prefer to poke around without Tom Mann for company. It would be more expedient simply to ask Mel Sweeten's widow for permission to take a look around the Dog Academy.

Jackie did accept Mann's offer to give Jake a free and immediate "obedience evaluation." She would take advantage of the interval to go on up to the Sweeten house and hear what Amy had to say. After all, a chance encounter with the widow and an opportunity to inspect the scene of the crime were really what she had come for. Michael McGowan hadn't *exactly* invited her to join his team of crack investigators; neither had he warned her off. Jackie decided that silence does indeed give consent. She left Jake with Mann and went to the Jeep to get a loaf of homemade zucchini bread, which she had brought with her as a small offering for Amy.

On her way up to the house, Jackie passed a small group of eight or nine fairly large enclosures, with a low, long shed running along the back. The dog runs, where Mel Sweeten had died. On one of the gates there was a yellow tape seal, bearing the legend CITY OF PALMER DO NOT BREAK in huge letters. The tape was all too familiar in its aspect. Jackie had last seen the seal of the Palmer police force on Philip Barger's office door, last fall. Seeing it here gave her a chill.

The last enclosure, the one nearest the house, was far grander than the rest. As Jackie got close she could see the reason why. Within, sleeping comfortably on bean-bag dog beds, were two large basset hounds, their foreheads a mass of heavy wrinkles, their ears spread like silky blankets over their front paws. These, she knew, were Mel Sweeten's pride and joy. One of the dogs looked up and sniffed the air as Jackie walked by; then it rested its massive head once more on its paws. Basset hounds really were cute, thought Jackie. They always looked to her as though they'd been designed by an upstart apprentice on the master artist's day off—all feet and ears and wrinkles and spots.

"I don't know what I'm supposed to do with them," said a voice. Jackie started. Amy had come up behind her very quietly.

"Let sleeping dogs lie," offered Jackie, feeling that it was a rather lame response. Even as she said it, the dogs awakened. They took one look at her and let out with an enormous, alarming noise, kind of a combination of a howl and a bark, deep and plaintive and somehow frightening. Jackie knew that bassets were fond of raising the alarm around strangers, but she hadn't counted on the deafening effects of a chorus of two.

Amy raised her voice to be heard. "They're supposed to be in a dog show today and tomorrow. Right here in Palmer, for a change, at the armory. Usually they have to travel."

"Well," replied Jackie, shouting over the noise of the bassets, "they look kind of tired. Maybe they need the day off."

"Yeah," said Amy Sweeten with a laugh. She began to lead the way across the lawn that separated the house from the Dog Academy. The dogs, watching the stranger retreat with the mistress of the house, quieted down. "Their fans will be clamoring for them," said Amy. "I suppose I have to figure out what to do with them. I don't know whether I should keep them. I would think that, technically, they will count as part of Mel's estate."

Yikes! thought Jackie. She had never contemplated dogs as constituting part of someone's estate. "Well, they *are* kind of cute," she ventured. One of the dogs had opened an eye halfway—just enough to give Jackie a heavy stare.

Amy shrugged. "Depends on your point of view, I suppose. I imagine that Mel thought they were cute too. Mostly, he thought they were worth a potful of cash. Fred's stud fee is something like a thousand dollars." On this strange note, she opened the kitchen door and ushered Jackie inside.

Jackie settled herself in the living room while Amy went off to the kitchen to make a pot of tea. She looked about her at the furnishings, which were for the most part well worn, in good taste, nothing special. But here and there a few items testified to Mel Sweeten's fondness for basset hounds. On the end tables on each side of the sofa were two lamps shaped like basset hounds standing up on their hind legs, their fat front paws playfully reaching up toward the light bulbs. Before the fireplace was a cushioned bench bearing a large sleeping basset on its needlepointed cover. There were ashtrays and nut dishes and other suchlike items scattered about, all bearing the likeness of basset hounds. And over a handsome table against a far wall was an enormous watercolor portrait, skillfully executed, of two bassets

sleeping, their blue ribbons dangling carelessly about their
fleshy necks.

Jackie, having taken in the basset touches of the decor,
began to study the house. After a look at the front door and
the hall beams she decided it was of the same vintage as the
clapboard "office" out back—probably just over a hundred
years old. It wasn't quite a farmhouse, and it wasn't really
a residence, either. It was an anomaly.

Something of her puzzlement must have shown on her
face, for as Amy came in with the tray and sat down, Amy
said, "Don't mind the dog lamps. And if you're wondering
about the house, it used to be a dormitory."

"Oh—of course. The James Lincoln Academy." Jackie
nodded. "I should have realized."

"When Mel's father bought up the old school property—
in the Depression, naturally, and for about three dollars—
he thought about doing a lot of different things with it. Had
all kinds of grand ideas, but according to Mel he was one
of those people who always have pipe dreams. In the end,
of course, he just sold most of it off, to developers. But he
kept the hockey field—that field where the training takes
place, where Tom is working with your dog now—and the
Briar Patch. That was what the girls at James Lincoln called
this dormitory. Because it was on the main road, and it was
so easy for the boys from Rumson Hill School to sneak over
in the night and kiss the sleeping beauties." Amy giggled.

Jackie didn't wonder at Amy's apparent high spirits. She
supposed that in four days the shock of finding her husband
murdered—or maybe it was the shock of having murdered
her husband—had not entirely worn off. Jackie knew that
it was often useful, in times of stress, to fix one's mind
on trivialities. If one could. So they made small conversation, about the James Lincoln Academy, and Mel's father's
grand schemes, and the school's final transformation into

Mel Sweeten's Dog Academy. At last, Jackie came to the point.

"I suppose the police have been here badgering you," she said.

"I would hardly call it 'badgering,' " replied Amy with a look of relief on her face. Perhaps she had been waiting for Jackie to broach the subject. "After all, he *was* murdered. But of course I can't tell them anything at all that's useful." She brushed back a languid hank of red-gold hair. "I wasn't here." She looked carefully at Jackie. "I know— well, everybody knows—that you were involved in the police investigation into Philip Barger's murder. That's why I wanted to talk to you. I was hoping you could tell me what to do next."

"Um—" Jackie began, but Amy held up a hand.

"You see, this is all foreign territory to me, and I don't have anything to judge it by. I've never been *in* a murder before. But you have. So I was hoping you could tell me how the police think, so I know how to respond. I don't have any references for this kind of thing."

There was something precise and scholarly about the way Amy Sweeten asked Jackie for advice. She might have been talking about evaluating a work by an unknown artist. In a way, thought Jackie, that was appropriate—her mind would probably take a scholarly approach to the problem, with her husband's death by violence as her primary resource material.

"I don't think I should try to advise you, Amy," Jackie replied. "Besides, other people's advice is never really much good. I never follow advice. The only good it ever does me is to help me see different sides of a question."

"All I can see is that I'll probably be arrested."

"Why do you think that?"

"Oh—lots of reasons. To start with, I don't really have a whatsit—an ironclad alibi for the time. I'd been over to Wardville for a couple of days, to visit my sister and look at one or two things in the museum there. They have a wonderful Eakins that I was hoping to photograph for our slide collection, but it was out being cleaned and so I couldn't get near it. So instead of staying until Thursday, as I planned, I came back here early on Wednesday. There were other things I needed to do. And that's why I found Mel."

Jackie gave what she hoped was a sympathetic nod, and Amy went on with her tale.

"The police think he died shortly after a meeting he had here with his doggy friends. I've heard that the meeting broke up around eight-thirty or so. They have those meetings every month, which was one of the reasons I went to my sister's house. I can't stand those dog people."

"No?"

"No. All they do is argue. So, anyway, the problem is that I went out on Wednesday night—I went out to supper, by myself, in Wardville."

"Somewhere nice?"

Amy Sweeten shook her head. "Denny's. My sister's kids were making so much noise that I couldn't concentrate on the notes I wanted to make. And the library was closed. So I thought if I just went somewhere by myself for a couple of hours, I could get some work done."

Jackie sympathized. It was difficult to concentrate with other people's children clamoring for your attention.

"But probably the people at Denny's will remember you, Amy," she reassured her colleague. "The person who took your order will remember you."

"I hope so."

"Besides, why would the police suspect you?"

"They think my behavior was . . . not right. The next day, when I came home, I mean."

"What happened?"

"Well, I was home by nine-thirty the next morning. By that time, I guess he'd been dead about twelve hours. But I didn't go out to the kennels, didn't find him until about eleven. I think that delay has made me a suspect. The police don't think it's reasonable."

Jackie considered this point. She knew some of the details already, thanks to her conversation with McGowan—and she knew that the time of death had been fixed for anywhere between nine and midnight. But Jackie also figured that such estimates generally included a margin of error of an hour or so. If Mel Sweeten had been killed at nine, Amy would have had time to drive the half hour from Wardville to the Dog Academy, kill her husband, and then drive back to her sister's house. But why would Amy want to kill her husband? She wondered if there was something that Amy was holding back.

"No," she said at last. "The police probably won't clear you entirely with that timetable working against you, until they have witnesses who can prove you were at Denny's." She looked Amy straight in the eye. "Did you kill him?"

Amy Sweeten looked scornful. "Of course not. If I'd wanted to kill him, I'd have done it long ago—with a little strychnine, or maybe Drāno, so he'd have suffered nicely."

"Oh." Jackie swallowed hard. This was hardly what she'd expected to hear.

"He had many characteristics that made him a really bad husband," said Amy, her voice strictly matter-of-fact. She might have been discussing a subject in a portrait—Henry the Eighth or someone. "He was fat, self-involved, boring, and adulterous."

"Oh!" said Jackie again, this time with more emphasis. She doubted that Henry the Eighth had been boring.

CHAPTER 7

"So, you see," Amy Sweeten was going on, in her matter-of-fact voice, "that's the other reason that the police might have thought I would want to kill him. Except they don't know about it, yet. Of course, they'll find out. And when they find out, and realize that I was holding out on them, then they'll come and arrest me. And, speaking frankly, I really don't have time for that. I have so much to do, and already I'm falling behind on my work, because I don't seem able to concentrate."

Good heavens! thought Jackie. Aloud she said, "Of course you can't concentrate. I would think that your best course right now would be to ask Dr. Westfall for a leave of absence for a few weeks, until things get straightened out." Dr. Westfall was B. Crowder Westfall, the dean of faculty at Rodgers University. "If you like, I can speak to him for you—he and I are on very good terms these days, even if I am only a rather mature instructor, and not a full professor."

Amy smiled thinly at this little academic jest, and then shook her head. "No, I really want to do my work. It's the only thing that's sustained me through the worst years of my life. I think it would be consoling now, if only I could pay attention."

Jackie took a deep breath and bit the bullet. "All right. So you haven't told the police, but you *have* told me, what kind of a husband Mel was to you. Want to tell me more?"

"Oh, sure. Now that he's dead I don't feel bad about telling it. Before, the whole thing made me feel kind of ridiculous. Inept. I didn't want people to think me inept."

She sighed and reached for another slice of zucchini bread. Mel's death had clearly improved Amy's appetite.

"We got married about two years ago. I was fresh out of graduate school—I had just gotten my master's degree—and Mel seemed sort of exciting, and different, to me. Well, you can imagine that he *was* pretty different from the kind of man I met in graduate school in art history. He was totally involved in outdoorsy kinds of things—in his dogs, and in dog shows, and everything to do with dogs. Not dogs—not just any dogs. Basset hounds. Those smelly, droopy ones out back that you think are so cute."

Jackie nodded. She really *did* think so, and found no reason to be ashamed of her feelings. In general, bassets were pretty adorable, and the ones out back were especially so.

"They've got fancy names, that they came with, but Mel called them Fred and Karen. As basset hounds go they're pretty important. Super deluxe champions or something ridiculous like that. Mel doted on them, and I suppose he loved them as much as he was capable of loving anything or anybody. He'd had a few others, before, that had been important too. In the dog world." Amy spoke contemptuously. "Mel's bassets have always been champions. They won all kinds of awards at dog shows, and he bred them and sold their puppies for a small fortune. Bassets have big litters. I would say Mel made quite a lot of money, over the years, thanks to Fred and Karen and others like them." Amy looked up at Jackie expectantly.

"So they were kind of the focus of his life," said Jackie. She didn't know what else to say. Mel Sweeten didn't sound like much of a prize. Jackie did her best to remember that this was his disillusioned young wife talking. Probably he hadn't been quite such a creep as Amy seemed to think. "I see."

"Do you?" Amy sounded skeptical. "Maybe. It was so strange, I tell you, to find that I had married a man who was totally consumed with basset hounds. I think they're sort of absurd dogs, anyway."

"I could see how you might want him to have at least one other interest." Jackie could sympathize a bit with Amy, who had married a man who seemed exciting and outdoorsy, but turned out to be a monomaniac. *Marriage always has surprises in store like that,* thought Jackie. *You marry the greatest man in the whole world, and then he turns out to be only, human, just a so-so kind of guy. If you were lucky, he wouldn't burn you and leave you scarred for life.*

But Jackie felt strongly that in fairness to Fred and Karen, someone ought to say something nice about them. Besides, they had just lost their master—and no matter what kind of a person Mel Sweeten had been, undoubtedly he had loved his dogs, and probably he had been very good to them. Today they had looked sort of sad to Jackie. But of course they were bassets, and bassets generally look a little forlorn. How would you ever know how they felt? Maybe they hated Mel, much as Amy seemed to have hated him.

In Jackie's mind, however, they deserved a strong defense. "But it's not their fault that Mel had a mania. I think they're sweet," she said firmly.

Amy nodded vaguely. "Well, most people do. I suppose I would too, if I hadn't had to live with Mel's obsession. Every weekend of the year, he was off at a dog event of one kind or another—either showing these dogs, or being a judge, or selling his puppies, or checking up on his puppies, or just hanging around looking at somebody else's. After a while, it really began to get to me."

Jackie could imagine that it might. Still, a man's hobbies, even if they bordered on mania, didn't usually provide people with an impulse to murder. Adultery, on the other hand, had been known to provoke.

"Um, Amy? You mentioned that Mel was, um—"

"Yeah." Amy nodded. "You wouldn't think he'd have time to look at women, not with so much energy devoted to breeding Fred and Karen to the right bassets, and with having to make so many trips all over. It never occurred to me, really, that he would. Or when I thought maybe he was, that she would be the one. I was surprised, frankly, that she could stand Mel. *That* way."

"Um, who's 'she'?"

"Sylvia. Sylvia Brown. She's an aerobics instructor, part-time, at a gym on the west side. And to pick up a few extra dollars, she hires herself out on weekends as a handler for dog shows."

"A handler?"

"You know—the people who take the dogs around in a circle in front of the judges at the dog show. On a leash."

"Oh. A handler. Huh—I thought the owners were the ones who did that."

"Sometimes they do. The real amateurs, usually, or the professionals who want to be seen or who don't trust anyone but themselves. But half the time at a dog show, especially a big one, the owners are really tense, worrying about their dog's performance, and they know things will go more smoothly with a handler. Or they don't have time to travel every weekend, and would rather not go to every dog show. Or if they're like Mel, really disgustingly competitive, then they spend their time trying to butter up the judges. Dog shows aren't really very nice, if you're one of those people. People like Mel. For them, a dog show's full of backbiting and intrigue."

"I had no idea," responded Jackie, who really was surprised. She had assumed that everyone—including the dogs—went to dog shows because they were somehow fun. She shook her head. It didn't sound like much fun at all. "So this woman, Sylvia, knew Mel through dog shows?"

Amy nodded. "She worked for him sometimes, showing Fred and Karen. Apparently she was just great with them, and they love her. Mel told me once that she seemed to get the best out of them."

"Do you know her?"

"Oh, sure. She used to come around here a lot—I guess until her guilty conscience got the better of her."

"Are you sure she was having an affair with Mel?"

"No. Well, I should say that I'm sure somebody was. Whether she was the only one or whether he had a whole string of them, I couldn't say. I think it was Sylvia Brown. You could say I'm convinced, but not actually certain."

"Why?"

"She seems like the logical person. She was just like Mel, about the dogs, I mean. Really into them, into their prizes. Every time she and Mel showed his basset hounds, or went to some dog thing, the animals seemed to come home with another ribbon or award or championship point. I don't know about you, but I can't stand the idea of giving dogs ribbons and awards and points. Even before I married Mel, I thought it was weird. Now I *know* it's weird."

"Well." Jackie wasn't quite sure how to respond. Surely the people at dog shows weren't all like Mel Sweeten— weren't all "disgustingly competitive," as Amy had put it. Jackie wasn't at all certain that Amy's idea of what was

weird and what was normal was something that the rest
of the world would understand. Amy seemed pretty weird
herself, if you asked Jackie.

But Jackie wanted to know more about Mel's supposed
affair with the aerobics teacher cum dog handler. Now,
that seemed like a situation with all kinds of possibilities. So she forged ahead. "It sounds just like a working relationship. Amy, why are you so sure that she and
Mel—"

"I just knew it. It had gone on for at least eight months."

"If you don't mind my asking, how did you know?"

"Well, first of all, there were the overnight stays after
the dog shows—perfectly unnecessary, most of the time,
but Mel would always say that he just had been too tired,
after two days of showing, to drive home on Sunday night.
Ridiculous. Then he'd turn up Monday morning, with new
ribbons and medals and photographs of those dogs to hang
in the office. Naturally I assumed something was going on,
but I didn't want to think about it, so I didn't. And then, of
course, I got the proof in the mail."

"The *what*?"

"Oh, some motel where Mel had stayed during a show.
They sent a package addressed to me—that is, to Mrs.
Melvin Sweeten—containing a black-lace nightie that was
definitely not mine, saying that we, that *I,* Mrs. Sweeten,
had left it behind in *our* room."

"Oh, dear."

"I suppose, in a way, they had done me a service. Before,
I had always looked at the situation from a totally personal
perspective—from the point of view of the person being
cheated on. It was offensive, but since I was the only one
seeing it, so to speak, I didn't think of it as an event, or a
series of events, taking place in the public view. I thought
of it as something having to do with *me*. That was a pretty

selfish viewpoint. The nightgown made me see the situation more objectively."

"What did you do?" Jackie asked, trying to keep her voice level. Clearly, "weird" was just the first in a string of adjectives that might be used to describe Amy Sweeten. She was either a deluded saint or martyr of some type, or a murderess. Or maybe some wacky combination of good and evil, like something out of a movie. Bette Davis and Paul Henreid in *Now Voyager*. Except Sylvia Brown would have to be cast in the Davis role. "When you got the nightgown, what did you do?"

"Well, of course I wrote back and thanked them, because returning it really showed it was a well-run motel. I thought they deserved a note. But the nightgown was too big for me. I would have been swimming in it—ridiculous. So I gave it to the St. Vincent de Paul thrift shop."

"No, I meant—well, never mind what I meant." Jackie was amazed. She couldn't really believe it—but on the other hand, she had never heard rumors that Amy Sweeten was crazy. Plus, from what little Jackie knew of the woman, she couldn't see her being happily married to a guy like Mel. It just didn't seem to fit. So it was possible that Amy had been just as cold-blooded about it as she sounded.

Or maybe it was a question of religious principles. The St. Vincent de Paul Society was a Roman Catholic charity, Jackie knew. Maybe Amy was Catholic.

But murder was at least as big a sin as divorce, so why murder him if you could condemn your soul forever by the simple expedient of paperwork?

Maybe murder would be appealing for reasons of economy, Jackie reasoned. Divorce lawyers cost money, as she well knew. Murder was cheap—at least do-it-yourself murder was. Almost free, in this case. The choke collar probably belonged to the Dog Academy.

Amy was going on. "As long as I didn't have to think about it too much, I could just pretend to myself that it was a passing thing. That he would get over it."

"Did you want him to get over it?"

Amy Sweeten considered the question for a moment. "Not really. Not at all. I think what I really wanted was to come home from the university some evening and find a completely different man here. A new husband, I mean. Someone thin and handsome, with eyeglasses, and an appreciation of what I think are the important things in life. Somebody who might go to a concert or museum with me, who knew something about things. Preferably someone who liked cats, rather than dogs. But I knew that it wasn't right to think that way."

Her voice had taken on a dreamy quality, and she paused, evidently imagining this prince charming, who sounded kind of dreary to Jackie. On the whole, Jackie thought she herself might have preferred Mel—if she'd had to choose.

Amy became businesslike as she picked up the tale once more. "I didn't like to be the one suggesting that we go back on our vows. That would have put *me* in the wrong, at least in my own mind. I was really just biding my time, waiting for him to tell me he wanted a divorce. Then it would be his idea, not mine, and the onus of breaking our vows would have been on him."

"Well, I don't want to split hairs with you, but hadn't he already broken those vows?"

"Sure. But he hadn't admitted it to me. Maybe the point was academic, but then so am I." She smiled sadly to herself.

Jackie decided that the best course, for the present, was to take Amy Sweeten at her word. The young widow hadn't mentioned her suspicions of Mel's affair to the police, but certainly, if Mel had been carrying on, they would find out.

If it was true, probably everyone on the dog-show circuit knew about it, or suspected it.

True or not, those suspicions now gave Amy a clear-cut reason to have hated her husband enough to kill him. If the affair had gone on for some time, the police would still consider those suspicions a good motive for murder.

"When did you get the nightgown in the mail, Amy?"

"What? Oh." She sat back in her chair and thought. "About two weeks ago."

Uh-oh, thought Jackie.

"I know—perfect timing," said Amy. "But, Jackie—I want you to believe me. I didn't kill him. Well, just *look* at me." She held out her spindly little arms, which seemed composed of bone and near-transparent flesh, and nothing else. Not a muscle anywhere. "I *couldn't* have. Not that way. For that kind of thing, you need to be in good shape. You'd have to be an aerobics instructor or something."

Jackie listened a little bit more to what Amy had to say. Amy had known next to nothing about Mel's business—after the first few months of marriage, she had realized that she would never be interested, so she had even stopped asking the barest polite and pro forma questions. All that Amy knew was that Mel made a lot of money, both from the Dog Academy and from his breeding. Tom Mann, Amy told Jackie, had been with Mel for at least ten years, maybe more. She filled Jackie in on some of Mel's friends and associates, but she really didn't know much more. Jackie had very little respect for women who lived in cocoons like that. At least Cooper, for all of his faults, had talked to her about the important things in his life.

Jackie soon made her escape, after first securing the widow's permission to take a look at the scene of the crime. Of course the dog run where Mel Sweeten had died—the one closest to the little office building—was still sealed off with police department tape. But Jackie wasn't interested in stepping in, and through the chain-link fence she was able to see as much as she needed to.

There wasn't actually all that much to look at; nonetheless Jackie stood contemplating the adjoining enclosures and the long, low shed running behind them for some minutes. The shed evidently was sort of a long doghouse with partitions; there were little doorways out of it giving on to each of the runs. The enclosures were about thirty feet long and ten or fifteen feet wide, with a gate at the end opposite the doghouse. There were eight enclosures, not counting the grander one where Fred and Karen still slept. A pretty small operation, the Dog Academy. And all of the dog runs were empty, except for the one with the bassets. Jackie wondered if business had been slacking off. Times were tough; in a recession, your dog's obedience-training budget has to be one of the first things to go.

Jackie looked up as Tom Mann approached, with Jake on his lead. The manager eyed her carefully as he turned over the end of the lead.

"Mighty nice animal, *Miz* Walsh."

"Oh!" responded Jackie. She had almost forgotten about Jake's evaluation. "You think so?"

"Yup. If I didn't know better, I'd think he'd had some pretty serious training somewhere."

"Was he good?"

Mann nodded. "Real good. Almost like he'd been trained by an expert." He gazed steadily at Jackie, who did her best to look proud and surprised. "He don't need a refresher course, *Miz* Walsh. He don't need anything. I wonder who taught him what he knows?"

"So do *I*," enthused Jackie. "Good boy, Jake." She patted him lightly on the head, and he gave her a bored look.

"See," Tom Mann went on, "I know he's never been here with us before. I'd remember him. But there aren't very many places around here where a dog gets a good training like that. And I'd remember him, if he'd been one of ours."

"Oh, well—"

"Because I have a memory for dogs. Like some people remember other people, I always remember dogs. Their names, and where they come from, who they belong to, things like that. Good for business."

"Yes, I guess it must be." Jackie kept her voice light. "But I'm pretty sure you're right, that Jake hasn't been here before."

"Nope. I'd have recognized him. Dogs like that don't come by every day." He stared at the dog. "Whoever trained him did a good job of it." He returned his gaze to Jackie. "If you find out where he got his training, you let me know, okay? I may be looking for a job, one of these days."

"Sure," said Jackie, trying to sound grateful and obliging. "Good boy, Jake," she said again, and took her leave.

She was glad to be getting away from Mel Sweeten's Dog Academy. As weird as Amy was, she at least had seemed manageable. Tom Mann, on the other hand, was an unknown quantity.

Squeaky voice or no squeaky voice, he was a big, beefy fellow. It would have been quite simple for him to pull hard enough on the choke collar to kill Mel Sweeten.

CHAPTER 8

Early on Sunday morning, sipping coffee quietly in the den, with Jake asleep at her feet, Jackie was still puzzling over her outlandish conversation with Amy Sweeten. It was almost impossible to believe that anyone could be so untouched by suspicions of her husband's infidelity. Yet precisely because Amy's attitude was so very odd, Jackie found herself wanting to believe in it.

Moreover, Jackie had no reason to doubt Amy's word that she hadn't murdered Mel. And she was of the firm opinion that Amy would not have had the strength, or the height, or whatever it might have taken, to slip a dog collar over Mel's head and about his throat and pull it tight. No— the crime had to have been committed by someone taller and stronger than Amy. Surely that much would be apparent to the police.

Jackie wondered how tall Sylvia Brown was. Amy had said the nightgown was far too big—the black lace number that Sylvia had left behind at the motel. Had Amy actually *tried it* on? Jackie shivered. A wife who could do such a thing was evidently superhuman in some way, or maybe subhuman. And they did say that people could develop superhuman strength to meet the challenges of extraordinary occasions.

Jackie roused herself from her thoughts, finished the coffee in her cup, and reached for the sports section of the *Chronicle*. Amy Sweeten had said that there was a dog show at the armory today. She looked up the schedule. The dog show started at eleven. The hounds were scheduled for noon, right after the sporting dogs. Presumably basset hounds went with the hounds, although they seemed sort of like sporting dogs, in a way, to Jackie, who had really no idea what was meant by "sporting dog," except probably a dog that you could take with you outside when you went out to have some fun. In that case, almost any dog would be a sporting dog, so probably that wasn't the criterion. Jackie looked at her watch. Plenty of time.

With a sigh, Jackie admitted to herself that she was behaving in a really nosy fashion. Yesterday's foray into police territory, unbidden, might be excused, although on very shaky grounds. But a trip to the dog show? That was sheer nosiness, and there was no way around it. She wanted to have a look at the mysterious woman whom Amy suspected of adultery.

Besides, the dog show *was* a public event.

What was more, Jackie could console herself with what she felt was a right to be nosy. After all, Amy Sweeten had confided in her, and was trusting Jackie to help her prove her innocence. Either that, or Amy Sweeten was a homicidal genius determined to make use of Jackie to clear herself. One way or the other, Jackie felt she was *directly* involved, and no apology would be needed for being seen to be intrusive.

Thus Jackie resolved to take a look around at the dog show. She rushed upstairs to her bedroom and threw on a pair of comfortable but respectable blue jeans, a soft maroon turtleneck, and a warm, knobbly, gray hand-knit sweater, which her mother had made for her. A visit to the

dog show wouldn't hurt, Jackie reflected as she brushed
her long, thick, dark hair and tied it back in a ponytail,
a style that she thought might be right for a dog show. She
put on a pair of earrings, to dress up the outfit somewhat.
If she caught a glimpse of Sylvia Brown, then she might
want to call Michael McGowan and fill him in a little bit
on her ideas.

As she stepped out into the brisk March air to walk the
fifteen blocks across town from Isabella Lane to Morrell
Street, Jackie gave some serious thought to her approach.
She realized that if she wanted to be any good at surrep-
titiously learning things about murderers, or about people
who could be murderers, she would definitely have to practice her technique. It had been very dismaying, yesterday,
the way the manager at the Dog Academy had seen through
her ruse. Of course, that had been partly Jake's fault—because he really was far too well trained to need any kind of
refresher course. Anyone but a perfect idiot could see that
at a glance.

Jackie, to slake her curiosity, didn't mind appearing like a
perfect idiot. But she had no illusions that such an approach
would work more than once. She would just have to play it
by ear.

If the Sunday morning traffic jam on Morrell Street was
any indication, the dog show apparently was a popular
event. The crowd of dog lovers who had turned up today
looked like a relaxed and fun-loving bunch. As she made
her way through the press of people gathered near the huge
arched front door of the armory, Jackie was on a careful
lookout for bared fangs, sneers, frostiness, and other signs
of the nightmarish competitiveness that Amy had described.
But all that Jackie saw was a healthy crowd of ordinary-
looking people, many of whom seemed to know each other

well. They greeted one another with hearty "hellos" and
heavy back-thumping; they inquired after one another's
animals, and they discussed the dogs that were going to
compete today.

The armory was a huge building, dating from the very
early part of the century. It was not only massive-looking,
from the outside, but also startlingly capacious, once you
got inside. It had once been the headquarters of the Fifth
Regiment, but that crack unit had been combined with another regiment from nearby Wardville, shortly after the First
World War. Ever since, the armory had been an invaluable
part of Palmer life. Its doorways were large enough to permit
the passage not only of tanks, but also of elephants; hence the
circus had always been held at the armory. High schools had
dances here, and groups of traveling acrobats swung from
the ceiling here. There were auctions and flower shows and
political rallies; and Jackie remembered significantly loud
rock concerts being held here, in her high school days.
The red brick must have intensified the sound of amplified
electric guitars by another two or three hundred decibels—
it was astonishing, really, that Jackie and her high school
friends had any hearing left at all.

By the standards of those days, the crowd that had turned
out for the dog show seemed small, quiet, and well man-
nered. Jackie entered through the main doorways on the
Morrell Street side. Straight in front of her, occupying
about one third of the floor space, was a large ring, in
which the dogs would evidently be performing. On the
right, covering about half the ring, were the grandstands—
Jackie recognized the old, splintery, green wooden benches.
They had been here forever. To the left of the ring was
an area that was evidently reserved for dogs and their
owners; it was separated from the entranceway by a large
picket fence, in white wood, that might have come out of

someone's backyard. At the far end of the huge room was a reviewing stand, evidently for the judges.

After about ten minutes of sizing up the layout and watching the crowd, Jackie decided on her technique. She would wander about in the crowd, selecting small clusters of people at random; then she would eavesdrop on their conversations, hoping to hear something about either Mel Sweeten or Sylvia Brown. If someone seemed to notice, she would just flash an innocent smile and simply drift away to the next cluster of dog lovers, trying hard not to be obvious.

Edging in this manner from one cluster to another, Jackie finally drew close to the ring, where the dogs being showed would shortly be called upon to exhibit their best qualities. Over to the left was the white picket fence separating the spectators' section from the area where the dogs and their owners awaited their big moments. From where she stood, Jackie could see what seemed like hundreds of carry crates and temporary cages. As she neared the gate in the fence, Jackie could sense the heightened tensions on the other side. Evidently the good-fellow feeling that prevailed among the spectators dissolved amid the anxiety of actually competing.

Jackie saw an argument shaping up right in front of her. Just on the other side of the fence stood a man of about fifty, with a toothbrush mustache and thick gray hair, and a stagily handsome face, as though he might once have been an actor. In one hand was a quivering mass of brilliant white, which looked to Jackie at first glance like some extraordinary small rat or weasel that had been held by its hindquarters and dipped in marshmallow fluff. On taking a second look, Jackie recognized the white mass as a poodle, with one of those decorative, pom-pommy haircuts that people seemed always to give them. The poodle's owner was scolding a red-haired, earnest-looking, firm-jawed woman of fifty or so. Evidently, the man felt that her beagle had strayed too close to the poodle's carry crate.

"*Some* people think they own a dog show. *Some* people think they can just *ignore* the rules, and *flaunt* the mandates of common courtesy," the man was saying passionately. Then he spoke gently to the little thing quivering in his arms. "Hush, Serena, my little flower, hush," he said to the dog.

The lady with the beagle reminded Jackie of Maggie Smith in *The Prime of Miss Jean Brodie*. The woman inhaled deeply and gave her dog's lead a stern tug. "Clematis wasn't in your way, sir," said the lady. "This is a public concourse." She nodded toward the poodle's crate. "Your box is over the yellow line. I certainly hope you won't attempt to make any foolishness over such a small incident. If you do, I shall see to it that your silly little dog never competes in this town again. The whole episode was in your imagination, anyway."

Clematis, the beagle who had been thus fiercely championed, tossed her nose into the air and sniffed merrily. Who could say, it might be her lucky day—there might be a convention of rabbits going on somewhere at the other end of the huge hall. She let out a short, sharp baying noise, a kind of a *brooop!* and was led away by her stomping mistress.

"Honestly," said the man with the poodle. He looked toward Jackie for sympathy. "She should *know* better. She does know better." He gave his poodle a comical look. "Feeling okay now, baby girl?" He smiled at Jackie. "Serena here isn't afraid of anything. But she knows how to lay it on thick at a show. Plus, her nerves are naturally just the tiniest

bit on edge, because the competition promises to be fierce."
He leaned across the fence to say in a low voice, "Believe it
or not, there's a woman here with the most *flea*-bitten bichon
frise. And she actually expects to win best in show." He was
deeply contemptuous.

"Oh," said Jackie, wondering what a bichon frise might
be. "Is that a kind of dog?"

"Well, of *course*, my dear." The man looked at Jackie
more carefully. "I take it you're not an aficionado of our
all-consuming diversion?"

"I really don't know anything about it—this is my first
dog show."

"Not really?" The man was scandalized.

"Afraid so. But I have a new dog, a very nice one, and
I was wondering what it would be like to show a dog—"

"What kind?"

"A shepherd. German shepherd."

"Oh, I think they're so nice, for working dogs. Don't you
agree?"

"I like ours," replied Jackie, trying to sound enthusiastic.
Working dogs, sporting dogs—to her, they were all just
dogs, and should do as they pleased. But she knew that
that attitude wouldn't get her far at a dog show.

"And he must be handsome," the poodle's owner went
on, "if you're thinking of showing him. Or is it a bitch?"

"A bitch? Um—no, no, he's a boy. A—a male dog."

"Good. They tend to be better in that group, I don't know
why. At least, so I think. But you were telling me—you've
never shown, and you came here today to see *what* this
madness is all about. Am I right?"

"That's right," Jackie lied.

"Well, then." Balancing the white poodle in one hand, he
fished in a pocket of his jacket and emerged, in a moment,
with a badge that said COMPETITOR/DAY 2. "Here." He held

it out. "I didn't bring a handler with me, and I don't have any cheering section here today, so it's extra. You can have it if you promise to cheer for us when we face our moment of truth. Put that on, my dear, and then you can come right on backstage here and see for yourself exactly who and what a bichon frise is, and anything else that might strike your fancy. Just be careful not to go too close to the carry crates, unless you like to make enemies fast."

Jackie grinned. "Thank you so much," she said, pinning the badge on her sweater.

"Unfortunately, you can't come in this way—you'll have to go all the way around to the other side, the Beadleston Street entrance, where they make you sign in and everything. But that's just as well, because this little thing"— he cuddled the dog—"and I have work to do. Just tell the dragons at the gate that you're with me—Phil Watts. Oh, Serena," he added, talking to the dog, "your hair is just a wreck." Serena was still, as far as Jackie could tell, a quivering mass of nerves. Hardly living up to her name.

Phil Watts smiled at Jackie. "We'll be on at about one-thirty. Wish us luck!"

"Of course," replied Jackie. "Thank you so very much!"

She made her way hastily through the growing crowd, around the back of the horseshoe-shaped grandstands, out one door onto Beadleston Street, and back in at the competitors' entrance. Doing her best to look like a professional of some sort, she flashed her badge and scribbled her name hastily in the logbook, then passed through to the competitors' side.

Preoccupied as she was, Jackie didn't notice that she was being observed. Across the way, almost hidden by the grandstands, Michael McGowan was watching her. On his face was an expression of mingled amusement and irritation.

It was only natural that an inherently curious and intrepid person like Jackie Walsh might turn up at the dog show today. But Michael McGowan was investigating a homicide—and so, clearly, was Jackie. Or at least she probably thought she was. Cosmo Gordon had warned him against trying to boss Jackie around, so McGowan was content, for the moment, to observe.

Nevertheless, he wasn't entirely happy that she had turned up here today. It had been one thing for Jackie to go around talking to suspects when the head of her department had been murdered. It was another thing altogether for her to be exposing herself to the dangers of a murder investigation in which she had no conceivable role. He wondered what on earth she was doing here.

McGowan moved out from under the shadow of the grand-stands and followed Jackie out through the back entrance of the armory onto Beadleston Street.

He had better keep an eye on her, for her own sake.

CHAPTER 9

Once she had crossed through the competitors' gate, Jackie was immediately aware that the atmosphere had changed. There were about fifty or sixty dogs competing today, she guessed—if the number of people and carry crates was anything to judge by. There were dogs of all colors, dogs of all shapes and sizes, being fretted over and cajoled by their owners. Some of the owners and their animals appeared to be taking it all in stride; others were clearly more nervous.

The large waiting area was broken up into six or seven large zones, in which dogs of a certain affinity were grouped together. Jackie stopped briefly near the front desk to look at a hand-lettered chart that indicated the layout. It seemed to her that the most logical place to start was with the hounds.

It seemed to Jackie, as she passed along the aisle where the dogs and their owners waited, that this crowd was really not all that friendly. She noticed that people tended to stare at her in a suspicious manner—those people who weren't all caught up in the anxiety of preparing their dogs, grooming them, and giving them last-minute words of encouragement or advice. There wasn't much bonhomie on this side of the white picket fence. Jackie tended to

associate dogs with lightheartedness, but there was nothing
lighthearted about the people here today. They were all in
deadly earnest.

She made her way past the terriers, who were all keyed
up, some barking incessantly, others merely giving off pal-
pable quantities of nervous energy. Then she wandered
slowly through the sporting dogs, who looked to Jackie
to be having more fun than anyone she'd seen so far. A
Labrador retriever was lying happily on the ground outside of his carry crate, chewing on a sodden mass. Closer
inspection revealed it to be an old tennis ball. Across the
aisle from the Labrador, two vizslas, obviously old friends,
were curled up asleep next to each other, making an inde-
terminate, soft-looking pile of velvety reddish fur. Next
to them, a golden retriever was being groomed, its head
proudly erect, its long fluffy tail a plume of feathered
sunshine. On the dog's face was the breed's customary
look of obliging cheerfulness. They made wonderful pets,
Jackie reflected. But then, so did Jake.

As Jackie looked up from the golden retriever, a movement on the other side of the aisle caught her eye. There was
a striking-looking blond woman about thirty yards away, on
the left. She seemed to be a familiar of the dog-show world;
as she walked by, people greeted her, and she nodded at
them and returned their salutations.

Jackie watched with interest as the woman left the main
aisle of dog crates and opened a large wooden door. This
door led into a back hallway that ran the length of the
armory's main floor; in Jackie's high school, rock-concert
days, the passageway had been notorious as a place where
you could find a little privacy with your date. According to
the layout map that Jackie had studied earlier this morning,
the dog-show judges had been given a room off the passageway in which they could relax between rounds.

Jackie thought fast. She had a feeling that this woman was Sylvia Brown, Mel Sweeten's handler. She could follow the woman innocently enough—the door apparently wasn't locked. The only difficulty was in figuring out how to sneak through the door without causing suspicion—undoubtedly, the judges' room would be off-limits to casual visitors.

Jackie soon found the perfect excuse. It was a large black dog, looking like an overgrown black poodle without a haircut, and it was waiting impassively in a large crate just in front of the door, at a considerable distance from the other dogs in the group. There didn't seem to be anyone around. It would be easy enough to pretend to admire this poodlelike dog, and then slip through the door after her quarry.

But she had no sooner crossed the aisle and approached the carry crate when she was stopped by a voice.

"Ma'am, if you please."

"Oh, sorry." Jackie stopped short and turned to face the man, embarrassed. She supposed it was the dog's owner; a short, round, middle-aged man with spectacles and a face that was all spherical lumps—a lump of a chin, lumps for cheeks, and a round lump of a nose. He looked as though he had been assembled from parts. "I just wondered what kind he is," she lied.

The man gave her an odd look, and Jackie was suddenly conscious of her badge. Competitors ought to know these things, she reasoned. "I'm strictly an observer here. Helping out a friend. In one of the other groups."

The man raised an eyebrow. "Well, if you're an observer, then maybe you don't know the rules. But the first rule of a dog show is you never, ever go near anybody's dog without being invited."

"I should have known," said Jackie, feeling truly embarrassed. She *should* have known. She would give herself away, and be expelled from the dog show, and never find out anything about Sylvia Brown, if she wasn't more careful about the regulations.

Jackie's ruefulness did the trick—the man seemed to relax a bit. "And the fact is, there's been a little trouble lately," he added, unbending.

"Is that so?" Jackie felt her nerves tingle. "What kind of trouble? Dogfights?"

"Oh, no. That happens, of course, but those little scuffles are easy enough to deal with. No, we had a tragedy a while back at a show near Philadelphia. One of the dogs competing was poisoned."

"How *terrible!*" Jackie was deeply shocked. "Did the dog die?"

"No"—the man shook his head—"but it was out of the show, and that was really upsetting to its owner."

"Maybe it was just sick, then," said Jackie. "After all, who would poison—"

"Oh, people go to all kinds of lengths to be sure they win their championship points." The round man shook his head.

"It wasn't *your* dog, was it?"

"Nope. A beagle. One of Thalia Gilmore's." He added this last bit of information in a voice edged with respect.

"Oh." The man seemed to expect Jackie to know who Thalia Gilmore was. It seemed that the criminal nature of the offense was heightened because the poisoned dog had belonged to Thalia Gilmore. Whoever she was.

"Now, this dog over here"—he gestured toward the poodlelike animal—"she wouldn't let anybody near her long enough to slip her poisoned food."

"What kind of dog is that?"

"An Irish water spaniel."

"She looks kind of cute."

"She may look cute, but she's pretty aggressive, especially with strangers, and especially on show days. That's why she's way over here."

"Are you her owner?" Jackie was now making conversation just to be polite. She couldn't very well sneak through the door to the judges' room with this man watching. But a glance at her watch showed that it was nearly eleven-thirty. She was suddenly impatient to reach the hounds, but she managed to keep her impatience under wraps.

"No, I'm her handler," the man answered. "Her owner's off on some yacht in the Caribbean right about now."

"Hmm. Listen," said Jackie eagerly. "I wonder—oh, you must be really busy."

"Not just now, no, I have a minute or two to spare." He gave her a curious look and folded his arms.

"Well, a friend of mine had suggested that I show my dog. But I don't know anything about it—about dog shows, that is. Then someone else told me about dog handlers, and I thought maybe that would be the way to go about it. Do you think I should try to find someone to help me show my dog?"

"What kind is it?"

"A German shepherd."

"Does your dog have papers?"

"Um, yes, of course." Jackie supposed that Jake had some kind of papers, somewhere. At least a diploma from the K-9 school, and probably something telling who he was and so forth. His records would be on file at the Palmer police. "He couldn't very well be in a dog show without papers, could he?" She flashed the man one of her working smiles.

"Well, not in this kind of dog show, at least," said the man, showing the first faint hint of a smile. He had begun to sound more agreeable. "So you'd like to find yourself a handler, you think?"

"That's right."

"Well, I tell you what you do." He reached in his back pocket and came up with a small folded pamphlet. "Get yourself a copy of this little publication." He held it out. *The Canine Chronicle* proclaimed the title. "It comes out once a month—it's on sale out in the front there, next to the grandstands, for a couple of dollars. Dog handlers looking for work tend to advertise."

"Oh," said Jackie. "You don't happen to know of anybody, just off the top of your head, who might be free?"

The man scratched his head. "Well, not really. Not for a shepherd. Except, now, wait a second . . . of course! I had forgotten. Terrible, just terrible. But you might want to try Sylvia Brown. The guy she used to do regular work for died, and she may be looking for new clients. I think she's probably here today."

Jackie took a small notebook out of her handbag and scribbled the name. "Is she good?"

"They say she's very good," replied the man with an odd chuckle. "She's been on the circuit a long time. You should look for her over in the hounds. You can't miss her. Blond, six feet tall, built like an athlete. Tell her Ralph Stevens sent you."

Aha! thought Jackie. But she merely smiled upon the man, thanked him for his time, and headed off toward the hounds.

Michael McGowan had prevailed upon the guard at the gate to allow him passage to the competitors' area, and he had spent the last half hour following in Jackie's footsteps, amused by her erratic progress. It was easy enough to see which dogs she liked and which she didn't. The non-sporting dogs didn't rate much of a look, except for a rambunctious dalmatian that was straining at his lead, and a very cute pair of Tibetan terriers, one golden and one black-and-white, both looking as though they'd do anything for anybody. McGowan had a cousin who raised Tibetan terriers. They were wonderful dogs, no question about it, although McGowan's cousin, who had a dozen of the boisterous little things, was a little overboard about them. People got that way about their dogs, though.

From next to the Tibetan terriers he had watched as Jackie made her way through the sporting dogs. Predictably, she had sped past the pointers but stopped to linger over the retrievers. Pointers, springer spaniels, and other tightly wound outdoor dogs were breeds that required deeper acquaintance to be appreciated; whereas the retrievers were everybody's pals, pretty much from the start.

Now McGowan himself was among the sporting dogs. He stood in a small group that had gathered around a phlegmatic-looking lump of a dog—someone had mentioned that it was a clumber spaniel—and watched Jackie's conversation with the Irish water spaniel man with interest. As Jackie ended her conversation and headed off at a brisk pace down the long aisle, McGowan detached himself from the clumber spaniel's admirers and began to follow. She looked to be heading straight for the hounds; evidently the man with the Irish water spaniel had told her something of interest. As he trailed her down the long aisle, McGowan made a mental note to tell Jackie to work on her poker face.

When Jackie reached the hounds area, there was no sign of anyone who might be Sylvia Brown. Jackie determined that her best strategy, for the moment, would be to try to pick up what information she could, before tipping her hand, by listening to the conversations about her.

She looked around, trying to locate a spot that seemed promising.

In the first carry crate there was an enormous blood-hound, sound asleep and snoring loudly, looking like a huge brown blanket of wrinkles. On a chair next to him was a man who—except that he was a man and not a dog—might have been a bloodhound himself. There were the same pendulous jowls, the same long, loppy ears, the same look of thoughtful assessment that you might see on the face of a working bloodhound. The man looked, too, like he might drop off to sleep at any moment. Then the resemblance between him and his dog would be complete.

Nothing doing here, thought Jackie.

The next spot was occupied by the beagle lady, whom Jackie had already seen engaged in a heated exchange with Phil Watts, owner of Serena, the poodle. The beagle lady looked like a more promising source of information—she was even now calling out to one woman across the aisle, while physically detaining another.

"I tell you it's just not right," the woman was complaining as Jackie moved close enough to hear. "Yooo-hooo! Virginia!" She beckoned to the woman from across the aisle. Then she turned back to her audience. "And I don't *care* if it was only a letter to the editor. Then it's the *editor's* responsibility as well. Dick Buzone ought to be disqualified from judging, just for having printed something so inflammatory, and so unfair. He positively maligns poor Clematis, and all of her sisters and brothers. He never knew a thing about beagles anyway."

"Oh, now, Thalia," said the woman whose wrist the beagle lady was holding. "Don't fly off the handle, will you? You *know* that if you lodge a complaint against Dick Buzone you'll only get his back up and make it worse for yourself." She patted the beagle lady's wrist and gently extricated herself from her grasp. "I must go, really. They're calling the non-sporting dogs, and just look at the time."

The woman addressed as Virginia arrived just as the other woman escaped. "Oh, Virginia. There you are," said the beagle lady. "Here, have you *seen* this outrage?" She waved a copy of *The Canine Chronicle* under Virginia's nose. "Have you *seen* what that man said about my dogs?"

"I *did* see it, Thalia," said Virginia, her voice warm and full of sympathy. "But if I were you I wouldn't let it worry you. After all, the man is dead."

Jackie perked up her ears.

"Yes. He's dead, but he lives on. An utter nuisance, in death as he was in life."

"Now, Thalia—"

"Besides which, I do *not* see the purpose that it serves to print such garbage. Dick Buzone should know better. I am going to circulate a petition to have him disqualified, Virginia, and I will expect you to sign it." Thalia Gilmore—for Jackie had concluded that this was she, the awe-inspiring woman whose dog had been poisoned in Philadelphia—folded her arms across her impressive front and glowered at Virginia.

Virginia, however, was apparently used to the beagle lady's tirades, for she neither acceded nor promised even to think about it. She merely changed the subject.

"Have the police been to see you yet, Thalia?"

Jackie, pretending to admire a saluki tied up across the aisle, moved in a little closer.

"Why on earth would the police want to see me?" retorted Thalia Gilmore.

"Well, after all, Mel *was* murdered. And you did see him that very evening, didn't you? At the meeting."

"He was alive when I left. They can't possibly think I had anything to do with that," sniffed Thalia Gilmore. "I wouldn't stoop to it. Wouldn't stoop. I'm surprised at you, Virginia, I really am."

"Well, you must admit that you and Mel had a quarrel brewing."

"Well, dear heavens, yes! He was such a provocative man. The way he treated my poor Clematis, the last time she stayed at that idiotic Dog Academy, was something else indeed. But I wouldn't murder him, when I could simply shun him. Far more effective." She lowered her voice to impart confidential information; Jackie could still easily hear every word. "He was banned, you know, from the Greater Palmer Bassets and Beagles Association, on *my* recommendation. That's why he wrote this tripe." She waved *The Canine Chronicle* again. "But Dick Buzone—he's another matter altogether. Printing this nonsense—especially after my tragedy in Philadelphia. Oh, the two of them were thick as thieves, but I am surprised that the murderer was so clumsy. Only did half of his job. To think, Virginia, that I'm a *subscriber*."

"You know that never makes any difference to Dick. Now, just calm down. Look at poor Clematis—she's all ready to go, Thalia, and you're a wreck. Comb your hair and put on some lipstick. They're ready for the hounds. You'll be on in five minutes."

Clematis, the beagle, did indeed look as though she was impatient to show off for an audience. She wagged her tail merrily and sniffed the air with a cheerful readiness. Thalia Gilmore, with a sniff of her own, withdrew an old powder compact from her pocket and began to powder her nose. The scent of the powder reached Jackie, reminding her powerfully of her childhood, of waiting for her mother to get ready. Jackie hadn't known they still made that kind of face powder.

Evidently Virginia's pep talk had worked. Thalia Gilmore,

in another minute, took a deep breath, squared her shoulders, gave Clematis's lead a sharp tug, and strode off toward the show ring.

Jackie looked at her program of the day's events. The judge for today's competition in the hounds was a man called Richard Buzone. Apparently, he was not very popular with the hound owners—if Thalia and Virginia's conversation was anything to go by. Jackie wondered how she might be able to approach him. But that would have to wait. First she must see if she could find and size up Sylvia Brown.

Finding her, now that the hounds and their owners were all concentrated near the show ring, proved to be a much simpler matter. Jackie soon saw her leaning up against a dog crate, her elegant arms folded, her pale thin hair cascading down her back. She seemed to sense Jackie's presence, for she turned around and gave her an inquiring look, then turned her attention once more to the ring.

She was indeed unmistakable, as the water spaniel's handler had said—six feet tall, at least, with long blond hair, a fresh-looking face, and a graceful way of moving. If Amy's suspicions were true, it wouldn't take much to imagine Mel Sweeten falling for her. Or any other man, for that matter.

Suddenly there floated into Jackie's mind an image of little Amy Sweeten trying on this Amazon's black-lace nightie—Jackie had to stifle a laugh, not of amusement but of horror. *Poor Amy!*

Now that she was face-to-face with the woman, Jackie was utterly at a loss. It was one thing to pretend to want to hire a dog handler; it was quite another thing to boldly march right up to the woman and make conversation. Especially in a setting like this, where everyone seemed preoccupied, with their minds very much on the events of the afternoon. What could Jackie hope to say? "Oh, by the way I wanted to know if you were having an affair with Mel Sweeten"? No, hardly. That wouldn't do.

There was another possible approach, however. Amy Sweeten had mentioned that Sylvia taught aerobics at a gym on the west side. It would be easy enough to sign up for a class, and then strike up a conversation afterward. That approach would be much more natural, Jackie reflected.

As these thoughts fluttered through her mind, Jackie was startled to hear a pleasant, familiar voice behind her.

"Miss Brown?"

Jackie turned around hastily. There was Michael Mc-Gowan. He gave Jackie a quick look that plainly said, "Play it cool." Jackie took the hint and kept silent, shrinking back a little way as McGowan dug out his identification. "I'm Lieutenant McGowan of the Palmer police department. I wondered if I might have a word with you?"

Sylvia Brown sized McGowan up with a quick glance. Then she lifted one side of her mouth in a smile. "You sure took your time about it." She gave her long hair a toss and moved closer to the detective. "Your place or mine?" she asked in a soft voice.

Jackie felt an unreasoning rush of something that felt suspiciously like jealousy. She stifled it, and managed to don an amused smile for McGowan's benefit.

"Oh, my place, I think. The view is spectacular." He smirked at Jackie and headed off, guiding Sylvia Brown gently by the elbow.

"That little worm," muttered Jackie to herself.

CHAPTER 10

"An apology?" said Jackie coolly into the telephone. "What on earth for?" She furiously stirred a potful of spaghetti sauce on the stove. She was still pretty annoyed with the way her afternoon's sleuthing had turned out.

"Oh, come on, Jackie," said McGowan. "I was just doing my job. Don't be that way."

"I'm not being any 'way,' Michael."

"Yes, you are. I called to apologize for acting like a schoolboy, or something, today."

"It's quite all right. You don't owe it to me to act like a grown-up." Jackie knew that probably stung, but it was true. Still, she really ought to come down off her high horse a bit. She genuinely liked Michael McGowan. "Oh, okay. You acted like a schoolboy, but I forgive you. Is that better?"

"Much. Don't you want to tell me why you were sneaking up on that woman today?"

"Of course I do." Jackie caught herself. "But I wasn't sneaking up on her."

"You were too. I followed you all morning, Jackie, and you were *definitely* sneaking. Hey, I snuck up on her too— it's nothing to be ashamed of, take it from me. So. When would it be convenient for me to come over and grill you?"

Jackie looked at the clock. Nearly suppertime. "How about now? But only if you promise that you'll bring a bottle of red wine for us and some ice cream for Peter. That is, if you want any spaghetti."

"Of course I do." McGowan sounded pleased with himself. "What flavor?"

"Hold on a minute." She covered the receiver and called to Peter, who was in the den with Jake. Chocolate, the answer came back, and was duly relayed.

"Is he your boyfriend, Mom?" asked Peter predictably when Jackie told him that McGowan was coming for supper.

"No, baby, he's not my boyfriend. He's just a friend. He's working on a case, and he thought maybe I could help him."

Peter looked suitably impressed. "Like before."

"Well, kind of. Not quite as much in our own backyard, but a man was killed last week, and I happen to know his wife. She works at Rodgers. So—that's all there is to it, really. Did you have an okay time with your dad this weekend?"

"Uh-huh." Peter clammed up.

Just as well, thought Jackie. It was infinitely preferable to her not to know anything about her ex-husband's activities, or to know as little as she could get away with.

Thus Peter and Jackie turned their attention to the spaghetti sauce, and then to making garlic bread and a salad. So that by the time McGowan got there, around seven o'clock, everything was ready. Peter was rather proud of the garlic bread, which he considered to be his specialty.

• • •

When supper was finished, and the chocolate ice cream was gone, Peter absented himself from the kitchen table to finish his homework (fractions), leaving his mother and McGowan to talk about the events of the day.

"Listen, Jackie," McGowan began in a solemn voice, "I don't want to be telling you what to do. But how was it that you turned up at the dog show in the first place? And why were you sneaking up on Sylvia Brown?"

Jackie smiled. It was kind of fun to mystify her detective. And she was curious to find out if the police suspected that Mel was having an affair. "I wasn't sneaking. And a dog show is, after all, a public event. I bought a ticket, just like everyone else."

He shook his head. "Jackie, really. You ought to trust me, you know. After all, it's not just a coincidence, is it, that you were spying on the woman who handled Mel Sweeten's dogs?"

"There's no law against going to a dog show, is there? Why did you come to grill me?"

"Because it's my job." Sometimes the simple truth was the best course. "Besides—you could get hurt. And I think that would be my fault."

Jackie pondered this. After a moment's thought, she nodded. "I appreciate that. Okay. I suppose, in a way, I got a little curious."

"A little curious?" McGowan laughed. "Any more curiosity and I'd have to swear you in as a deputy. Now—spill it."

Jackie took a deep breath and told him about her visit to Mel Sweeten's Dog Academy. He was vastly amused by her cover—the attempt to sign Jake up for a refresher course in obedience training.

"I tell you, Michael, I didn't really have a comfortable feeling about that manager, Tom Mann. He gave me the creeps. Have you checked him out?"

"We have. He was away on vacation all last week, in Florida."

"Oh." Jackie was disappointed. "Maybe he came back early?"

"Nope. Well, we're double-checking, of course. But I imagine his story will hold up. You can't fudge that kind of thing for long. At least, you can't lie to the police about it."

"Oh. No, I guess that would be pretty stupid. But frankly, Michael, I don't think Amy Sweeten could have done it. For one thing, she told me that she didn't."

He grinned. "Did you expect her to say that she had?"

"No—but you never know. She's kind of an odd person. She—well, since you were sneaking around at the dog show, I guess that means you know, um, something about Sylvia Brown?"

"Oh, yes." McGowan teased her with a grin. "Not that I wouldn't like to know more. But we're working on the relationship between Sylvia Brown and Mel Sweeten, if that's what you mean."

"I guess maybe that's what I mean." Jackie felt great relief. She hadn't wanted to violate a confidence. But Amy hadn't actually asked her to keep anything confidential—in fact, that was sort of odd, when you thought about it. Jackie was suddenly overcome with the certainty that Amy had wanted to use her as a conduit to the police. For embarrassing information that it would have been too difficult to pass along on her own initiative. She furrowed her brow.

"What?" asked McGowan.

"I wonder if I'm being used," replied Jackie.

"Of course you are. I'm using you right now, as a sounding board and a source of information. If that man's widow talked to you—and I think she probably bent your ear—then it's a sure bet she wanted you to talk to us."

"How do you know?"

"Because." He leaned forward and rested his arms on the kitchen table. "When I turned up there to talk to her last Thursday, she said she knew that you and I were friends."

"Oh!" Jackie sat back in her chair.

"So—forget all about the seal of the confessional, and tell me what you think."

"Okay." Jackie took a breath and related to him most of her interview with Amy Sweeten. She omitted any mention of the nightgown, out of a desire to protect Amy's weirdness from the bald scrutiny of the police. Nor did she say that Amy suspected Mel of cheating on her, but McGowan had already drawn that conclusion.

"Did she mention anything about a nightgown?" he asked.

"Umm—" Jackie hesitated. "A nightgown?"

"Yeah—a little lace number from Victoria's Secret," he told her as Jackie hesitated. "We know all about it. The motel manager called us Friday morning, after reading about the murder in the paper. Seems someone calling herself Mrs. Sweeten, who had booked a room at his place for one night, left a nightgown behind. So he mailed it back to her. Then about a week ago he gets a thank-you note in the mail. Very punctilious, you might say. But he thought the note was kind of odd, because Mrs. Sweeten asked the manager to write back and confirm the date on which she had stayed at the motel."

"Yikes," said Jackie.

McGowan grinned. "I agree. The manager thought that was pretty weird, and when he read about the murder he thought he ought to tell us. Wanted to be a good citizen. Which just goes to show that cheating husbands never seem to learn."

Jackie ignored the jest and McGowan seemed to sense that he had stepped on a sore point, because his expression quickly grew somber again.

"So, Jackie, here's what I think. Off the record, of course. I think Mel Sweeten was having an affair. Maybe with Sylvia Brown, maybe with someone else. From the police point of view, you know, that's a pretty strong motive for murder. Tried and true, anyway."

"I suppose so," agreed Jackie reluctantly. "Okay, suppose Amy did have an idea about it. She still probably wouldn't kill him. She wanted him to divorce her." She told McGowan briefly about Amy's waiting game. "I admit that her logic about sticking around seems thin, but then people do cling to straws. Besides, I don't see how Amy could have done it. She's not nearly tall enough to sneak up behind a six-foot man and throw a choke collar over his head. But Sylvia Brown is plenty tall enough."

"Tall, yes." McGowan grinned again. "Okay. Personally, based on my interview with the victim's wife, I'd have to say that she doesn't look like she's strong enough to swat a fly. But we have to look at a few other things too, like opportunity and motive. The motive is big as all outdoors."

Jackie shook her head. "No, I disagree. She told me plainly that she might have wanted to murder him, but if she had she would have made sure he suffered. She was quite remarkably matter-of-fact about the whole idea."

"Most murderers are."

"Yes, but, Michael—if she had done it, why kill him right there at home? Why not do him in on one of his road trips? Besides, she says she was at a Denny's in Wardville, having dinner." Jackie rolled her eyes. "Now, if you were dreaming up an alibi, would you come up with something as dweeby as that?"

"Yeah, you have a point," McGowan conceded. "Okay, here's the story as far as we know it." He filled Jackie in a little bit on the meeting of the executive committee of the Greater Palmer Dog Fanciers Association. "At about a quarter to eight, there was some kind of racket outside—the dogs were barking their heads off, I guess. Sweeten went outside to check it out, and came back in again about ten minutes later. This guy Buzone thinks he was upset about something. Figures maybe there was a prowler trying to steal the dogs. And that Sweeten went out again later, after the meeting was over, and caught the guy red-handed. So the guy killed him."

"Strangling him with a dog collar but leaving the dogs behind? Come on, Michael."

"It's not *my* theory," he said defensively.

"Then what happened?"

"The meeting broke up at about eight-fifteen. Apparently it wasn't a friendly meeting—they had been arguing about something, but according to Dick Buzone, the president, the monthly meetings were always like that."

"I hate meetings," put in Jackie. "What were they arguing about?"

"Who should be the sponsor of the blue ribbon at the dog show. Not the sort of thing you ordinarily would kill somebody over."

"These people are anything but ordinary, Michael. Did you get a load of the decor out at Mel Sweeten's place?"

McGowan chuckled. "The dog lamps and dog ashtrays? Yeah, nice touches, eh? But I still don't think that passions about a dog-show sponsor lead to murder. And as far as we can tell, that's all that was discussed at the meeting."

"Do you believe that?"

"I don't know, really. No, I'm sure they talked about other things. But Buzone says they had a pitched argument about who the sponsor should be. The company that won out is McKean Pharmaceuticals."

"Doesn't sound very promising," agreed Jackie.

"Besides, let's look at the wife's motive again. She's off in Wardville, but that's only half an hour from here. She says she went to Denny's—but what if Amy Sweeten came home a day early and surprised Mel in the embrace of Sylvia Brown?"

Jackie shook her head. "Nope. If she came home and surprised them in an adulterous embrace, your blond bombshell would be a witness."

"She's *not* 'my' bombshell." McGowan fidgeted in his chair. "Okay, let's say for the sake of argument that Mel Sweeten was having an affair. With whoever. Doesn't matter. Say Amy comes home a day early, sees them, but they don't see her. Then the other woman leaves, Amy kills the husband, and then drives back to Wardville. Nobody, by the way, can vouch for her at Denny's."

"That's hardly surprising. The woman is practically invisible, she's so little and pale and skinny. No." Jackie was firm.

"You have to admit the thing about the nightgown is weird," said Michael. "Right? You admit she's weird."

"Look." She leaned across the table, intent. "I admit she's a weirdo. But this is what I think. She's trying to cope with the shock of being actually *glad* that her husband is dead. She's thrilled, like the Munchkins, you know, when Dorothy's house lands on the Wicked Witch of the East."

McGowan scowled.

"Well, then, like—like—" Jackie fished around.

"Like the wife in *Double Indemnity*."

"Right," said Jackie. "Like Barbara Stanwyck. She's delighted. She feels absolutely no regret at his death— and she's ashamed of her reaction, maybe, because it's not how she'd imagined it would be. Not how she'd always expected her marriage to turn out." Jackie colored slightly, but McGowan didn't appear to notice it. "You know, you have these ideals, and then the guy's a bum and you're— you're glad he died. But naturally if you have any sense of what's right and wrong, you're ashamed of that."

McGowan conceded that Jackie's logic had some strength to it.

"The way I see it," she went on, "there are some other possibilities. You wouldn't believe all that I saw and heard today at the dog show. Those people are worse than university faculty members for sheer internecine nastiness."

McGowan nodded. "So I gathered from my interview with Sylvia Brown. She told me it's a nest of vipers, the dog-show circuit. Of course, they close ranks like crazy when confronted with an outsider. You gotta have a dog to belong. Which is one of the reasons I wanted to talk to you. I want you to do me a favor."

"Oh?" Jackie smiled, interested. Evidently McGowan's territoriality didn't extend to things he couldn't easily do for himself. She would teach *him* to stroll off smugly with tall blond suspects.

He shrugged. "Well, I have to admit you gave me the idea. What would you think about sending Jake back to work?"

"Aha." Jackie frowned. "You mean that the Palmer police want him back?"

"More or less." McGowan could see that the idea wasn't going over very well. "Just for a little while, so that we can use him to get next to some of those dog people when they don't have their guard up."

Jackie glared at him. "I can't believe what I'm hearing."

"Why not? He's used to police work, you know. It's not

as though it would be hard for him."

"Maybe not for him—but how about for us? Haven't you got some other dog you could use?"

McGowan shook his head. "I tried that already. Spoke to Cornelius Mitchell about it—he's the guy in charge of our K-9 outfit. But no—remember the shipment of cocaine that came into the airport last week?"

Jackie nodded. "They're busy on that, I suppose," she said. "Noses to the grindstone."

McGowan chuckled. "A shortage of dogpower, that's all." He gave her a pleading look. "It would only be for a little while, Jackie."

"No."

"No?"

"No. What if something happened to him? Besides, they're sure to smell a rat, those dog-show people, if you send some of your big fat flatfoots around. So it would be a pointless exercise. They'd be on to you in two minutes."

"No way," protested McGowan.

"Yes, they will too. There were two of those guys at the Dog Academy on Saturday, and I knew at a glance they were yours. They stick out, Michael."

"Oh." He sounded disappointed. Jackie realized that she might have hurt his feelings—detectives were supposed to be good at undercover work.

Jackie grew thoughtful. "Here's a compromise," she said at last. "You can have the services of the finest ex-police dog in Palmer if you agree to let me be the one to handle him."

"Oh, come on, Jackie—"

"No, Michael. Either that, or forget it."

"But, Jackie, he's kind of not yours. I mean—is he?"

"Fine." She glared at him. "Go ahead, take him away right now, for good." Her eyes filled with tears. "Because either he's our dog or he belongs to the police. If he's ours, Peter's and mine, we'll be glad to help you on our own terms. If he's your dog, then go ahead and take him away, but don't you dare come back again. Anything else wouldn't be fair to me, or to Peter, or to Jake."

McGowan didn't have to think about it very long. "A deal," he said, "under one condition. And that is that if things get rough, or if you learn something important, that you tell me right away, and that you do what I say."

"Fair enough," said Jackie, who had no illusions about her own native ability to cope with murderers. She would leave that to the professionals—to McGowan, or to Jake, as the case might be. She stuck out her hand, and they shook.

"Now." Jackie rubbed her palms together. "Where do you think we should start?"

McGowan considered her question for a moment. "Now that people have seen you at one dog show, maybe the thing to do would be to go to the next one in the area."

"That's not for another month, Michael." She wrinkled her brow at him. "The schedule was right in the program. Honestly, don't you detectives detect anything?"

"I guess not." He grinned, trying hard to look humble.

Jackie tossed her long, dark hair. "If you hadn't been so busy sneaking around—"

"I was too busy," he admitted, contrite. "Sneaking is very hard work sometimes."

"But I have another idea." Jackie sat forward, alert. "Why don't I just pretend to be interested in signing up for a dog show, and kind of interview some of the leading competitors from the area. How about that?"

"Great," he said sarcastically. "Or maybe you should just tell them you're writing an article for your high school paper."

"It's not *such* a dumb idea," she retorted.

"Of course it's a dumb idea."

"Oh. Well, maybe it is dumb. Have a better suggestion?"

"No."

"Okay. Then we'll go with my dumb idea. And I think I know where to start."

"Yeah?"

"Yes. With one of the judges in the dog show. Dick Buzone. From what I could gather, everyone hates him. Did you hate him when you interviewed him?"

"I didn't exactly warm up to him. He's sort of like a flounder or something. Cold and pale."

"Well." Jackie grew enthusiastic. "I heard some old battle-ax saying that he and Sweeten were thick as thieves—but she just had a bee in her bonnet. She hates Mel Sweeten. Hated."

"If she's so full of ill feeling, why don't you start with her?"

"Nope. She hates Dick Buzone too. So, if I start with him, then I can move on to her, and we can both hate him together."

"Perfect."

CHAPTER 11

At a glance, Jackie guessed that it might be extremely easy to hate Dick Buzone. She disagreed with Michael's description, however; he was more like a long, thin eel than a flounder. He was cold and pale, definitely, and thin, with the kind of ascetic thinness that seemed to be a reprimand to people who like to eat. In his presence, Jackie was instantly conscious of the french fries she'd had for lunch. His lips were thin too—pale little lines of flesh that nearly disappeared when he closed his mouth. His eyes were pale amber, half-hidden by lids that reminded Jackie of the chameleons she'd had as a child. His hair was the only part of him that wasn't thin; it was dense, wavy, and the color of wheat. Jackie thought the hair was unjust. There were lots of agreeable and deserving men his age who would have given a potful of cash for a head of hair like that. It sat upon his head like some outlandish trophy. He was an eel with hair.

It was lunchtime on Tuesday, and Jackie had prevailed upon Dick Buzone to give her some advice about showing dogs. This much had been easy. Amy Sweeten had told her that Buzone was the president of the local dog fanciers club, and that he had been at the executive committee meeting at her house the night that Mel was killed.

Amy had also told her that if you wanted to break in to Palmer's dog world, you had to talk to Buzone. Mel used to laugh about it, Amy told her. It was almost as though Buzone thought he should interview people before allowing them to join his little circle. Amy, however, had never heard of anyone's being turned away. The membership dues, Jackie soon discovered, were thirty dollars a year, payable by check made out to Richard P. Buzone.

Now as Jackie sat conversing with him in the small office adjacent to his house, where he worked as an advertising consultant, and where *The Canine Chronicle* was published every month, she wrestled with the feeling that he was on to her. She had handed over her check and duly registered herself as a member of the Greater Palmer Dog Fanciers Association; in exchange, she had been given a bumper sticker for her car ("Show Dog On Board!") and a membership card. All that remained was to try to sound him out about Mel Sweeten.

"Well, I imagine that our chances are slim," she said, her voice sounding artificially bright in her own ears, "because I'm a novice, and our dog *is* getting on in years. But even if he doesn't win any prizes, I thought it would be nice to join. For my son's sake as well."

"Yes, indeed," said Buzone, studying her check carefully before tucking it away in a small safe behind his desk.

"But you're experienced," Jackie went on, "so probably you can tell me. Do you think a dog of advanced years has any chance of becoming a champion?"

"Depends on the dog," was Buzone's reasonable reply; somehow he managed to make it sound like a put-down.

Jackie controlled her defensive impulses and forged ahead. "He's very well trained, and he's beautiful to look at."

"Yes, I'm sure." Buzone shifted restlessly. "Look, Mrs., um—"

"Walsh. But please, call me Jackie. Everyone does."

Buzone looked at her. Clearly, he was not "everyone." He cleared his throat and continued. "Dog shows aren't for the fainthearted. It takes a great deal of dedication, and a great deal of time; even given the application of hard work, earning championship points also requires an outstanding dog. If you are only casually interested, I would suggest that you begin with obedience competition for your dog. You said he was a German shepherd?"

Jackie nodded. "What's an obedience competition?"

"It's a growing field," he replied, dismissive. "A less exacting type of competition, in a certain way. Obedience trials test a dog's readiness to perform certain tasks, and his ability to carry through with his job. Not more than that."

To Jackie, these sounded like things that might be more important, after all, than mere appearance. But she bit her lip as Buzone continued.

"An obedience competition does not test a dog's conformity to the breed's standard—and that, after all, is what we look for when awarding championship points to a dog. So if your dog is in any way short of the mark—which he probably is, most dogs are—you can still enjoy participating in a group event, get to know some people hereabouts—you said you were new to Palmer?"

Jackie nodded again. Another white lie for the scoreboard; she had grown up here, after all, even though she and Peter had only recently come back.

"Yes." Buzone was brisk. "Well, you'll find that at obedience competitions there are plenty of interesting people who attend. You will find it an easy matter to break the ice. It's not quite such a tense affair as a standard dog show. More of an outing."

"That sounds like fun," said Jackie, lying again. If there was anything that didn't sound like fun, it was a group outing with a bunch of dog nuts, watching their pets fetch and sit and jump and heel. "But I wouldn't know where to begin, really, with something like that. It doesn't sound much like an amateur's event. Do you think I need to hire someone to help me?"

"Ah, you mean a handler." Buzone considered this question, folding his lips inward until they became invisible, and his mouth was just a seam between his nose and his chin. He gave the freckled tip of his nose a businesslike tug and looked at Jackie with his pale eyes.

"I don't see why not, if you would feel more comfortable. As it happens, I know a very able young woman, about your age, who might be free to help you. She was regularly employed as a handler by one of the finest breeders in the area, but unfortunately their working relationship has come to an untimely end."

"I see," said Jackie, racking her brain desperately for a follow-up. "I think maybe I heard something about that, at the show on Sunday."

"Oh? You were there?"

"Didn't I mention that? That was how I found out about the Dog Fanciers Association. I spent most of Sunday at the show, because I wanted to see what one was like."

"I see." He stirred in his chair and tugged at a shirt cuff. "Yes, we observed a moment of silence at the start of the hound class in memory of Melvin Sweeten, one of the most outstanding men in our field."

Jackie nodded soberly. A moment of silence. Well, she hadn't noticed it, but then perhaps nobody had told the dogs that they had to stop barking and yapping. "He—he was *murdered,* wasn't he? And the police think his wife did it."

"Oh?" Buzone's pale amber eyes lit up. "I didn't know they had a suspect."

"Well, at least that's what I heard. But maybe it's just a rumor."

"The newspaper indicated that she was out of town at the time."

"Oh? I didn't know that."

"Yes. Out of town." Buzone shifted in his chair and tugged again at the tip of his nose. It must be a sign of interest, thought Jackie. He really was a repellent man, although she couldn't have said exactly why she disliked him so. But she was now eager to be gone.

"May I ask where you heard this information about the police interest in Mrs. Sweeten?" he inquired, sounding casual. "Her husband and I were longtime friends, and I'd like to be helpful to her if I can. Who told you the police suspected her?"

"Oh—I don't really know, actually," said Jackie evasively. "I think maybe I heard some people talking about it at the dog show."

"I'm surprised I didn't hear the rumor myself." He crossed his long, skinny legs and regarded her thoughtfully. "Are you certain?"

"I don't know how *I* could be certain of anything about it," replied Jackie reasonably. She was certain, however, of one thing—that Dick Buzone was displaying a great deal of interest in the matter. "I didn't even know the guy."

"No." He sniffed and raised an eyebrow. "No, so you didn't." He rubbed his dry palms together, making a chuffing noise, and reached into a drawer of his desk. "Well, then. Thank you for your interest." He regarded a small white card that Jackie had filled out. "Would you rather have your home number listed in our little directory? Or your office number?"

"Oh, the home phone, I think."

"But you do work?"

"Yes. Yes, I'm teaching film history at the university."

"Ah. Mrs. Sweeten is one of your colleagues, then."

"I know. There's been some talk on campus—but she's an art historian, and I deal with popular culture. You know that those are two very different worlds." *Lies number three and four,* thought Jackie.

"Yes, I suppose they are different. Ahem. Well, now. Why don't I give you this form to fill out"—he handed her the paper—"and you can submit it next weekend, for entry to our first obedience trials of the season. It's good fun."

Jackie sincerely doubted that anything with Dick Buzone could be good fun, but she dutifully folded the paper away into her pocketbook and thanked him. "About the woman?"

"What woman?" snapped Buzone.

"The one that you said might want to be a handler for me. For my dog."

"Oh, yes of course. Forgive me." He drew a single large sheet of blank paper toward him and picked up an expensive-looking fountain pen from a tray on his desk. "Her name is Sylvia Brown, and although I don't have her home telephone number, I'm sure she's listed. During the week, she teaches some sort of class at a gymnasium. This is the address. You will probably find her there, most evenings."

Jackie thanked him again and rose to leave. "Oh, one more thing," she said. "I almost forgot. You probably need my address. For the newsletter."

"The newsletter?" He didn't look pleased.

"Well, yes. I mean, isn't a subscription part of the membership?"

"Oh, no. *The Canine Chronicle* is quite a separate operation, Mrs., um—"

"Walsh." Jackie tried not to sound impatient.

"Yes. We don't sell subscriptions to the *Chronicle*—just single issues. Haven't got the manpower to mail it out—or the revenues, I'm afraid. But you'll find it on sale at the important shows, of course."

"Oh." Jackie let disappointment register on her face. Better that than puzzlement.

"Although," said Buzone in an expansive tone, "maybe we should give a thought to including the first copy free with paid membership. That's not a bad idea. Here you go." He reached around behind his desk and grabbed the most recent issue. "Gratis. For giving me the idea."

"Thank you," said Jackie, looking over the little magazine. "I appreciate your time."

"You're most welcome." Buzone was ready for her to go.

Jackie, for her part, was glad to be leaving.

CHAPTER 12

"Michael, why is it that every time you call me you apologize?" Jackie was in her office, between classes, looking over her standard lecture notes on the comic films of Harold Lloyd and their significance in the sociocultural setting of the twenties and thirties. The class would see *The Freshman* today. Jackie was pretty tired of *The Freshman*—one way and another, she had seen it about thirty times. She was aware, however, that very few comedies stood the test of time so well. So she resigned herself, and flipped through the note cards, and chattered away to McGowan.

"I don't expect you to be at home every time I call," she said. "And you certainly don't have to apologize to me for being out. That's what answering machines are for."

"Okay," said McGowan, sounding relieved.

Perversely, McGowan's eagerness to put things right with Jackie made her curious. For the first time, she felt that she *might* like to know where Michael McGowan had been last night, and with whom. But it wouldn't do to have that kind of feeling—that sort of thing would deliver her right into his hands. She dismissed her curiosity and grew businesslike.

"I only wanted to report on my conversation with Dick Buzone—the one you think is a flounder."

"Oh, yeah. Did you talk to him?"

"Yup. He's creepy. I think he probably did it. He's got yellow eyes. Icky."

"I agree that he's icky," McGowan said lightly. "Probably I should arrest him just for his ickiness."

"Well, you probably think I should go fly a kite, but I feel strongly that it's my duty as a citizen to tell you something about him."

"Like what?" McGowan sounded bored.

"Like this. He puts out a little monthly magazine that's on sale at all the dog shows. It's mostly ads, and then a few stories about things like dog hairstyles, or a new kind of chewy bone, or something." Jackie was fishing desperately in her bookbag for her copy of *The Canine Chronicle*; at last she found it and hastily flipped it open. "Here's one, in this month's issue, called 'Puppy Cuts for Older Poodles.' "

"Terrific. And?"

"Well, and this. At the dog show on Sunday I heard some old bat with a beagle say she was a subscriber. But Dick Buzone told me they didn't sell subscriptions."

"Jackie, that's hardly a clue."

"Oh." Jackie was stung. "Well, you don't have to sound so superior about it."

"I'm not being superior," McGowan protested.

"I thought it was kind of suspicious. I mean, there I was with my checkbook in my hand, all ready to fork over significant dough for a newsletter about *dogs,* for Pete's sake. And Dick Buzone says no, he's terribly sorry, but they don't take subscriptions."

"I don't see what's so strange."

"It's strange because I *know* that this lady with the beagle had a subscription. I heard her say it. Plus, I wondered how Mel Sweeten had gotten himself involved in the magazine. He had an article in it that the beagle lady was complaining

about. The beagle lady, for your information, was very
angry with both Mel Sweeten and Dick Buzone. And I
think she's a very important person in the dog world. Her
name is Thalia Gilmore." Jackie was rather proud of this
bit of information, but McGowan's response took the wind
out of her sails.

"Ah, yes—the one that's like a great tank."

"You know her?"

"She was one of the people there at the executive committee meeting. But Buzone saw her leave, and she has an
alibi for later on that evening."

Jackie hid her disappointment. "Oh, well. How's the
investigation going on your end?"

"Uh—not nearly as well. While you've been befriending
suspects, all of my people have been coming up empty-
handed."

"No evidence who the nightgown belonged to?"

"Not so far. We're tracing it, but it will take a few
days. It came from Victoria's Secret, we know that. But
it could have been a mail-order number. It will take a
while."

"You still think Amy did it, don't you?"

"I never said I thought that Amy did it."

"Oh, Michael. You didn't have to say what you thought."

"Oh."

"Hey, listen. When you were at the dog show on Sunday,
did you happen to watch any of the competition?"

"A little bit, when I wasn't hunting for suspects or sneaking around with Sylvia. Why?"

"Well, it just occurs to me that you and Bathsheba—
I mean Sylvia—sneaked off right about the time that the
hounds were competing."

"Yeah, I was really sorry to have to miss the big sniff-off
in the center ring. So?"

"Well, so—be sensible, Michael. Bassets hounds are *hounds*."

"No, really?"

"Boy, you are being snide today. What's gotten into you?"

"Nothing. I just don't get the excitement about the hounds, that's all."

"Well, you and I are not dog nuts. Thank heavens. But those people are really serious about this stuff, Michael. I think you ought to talk to somebody called Frank Dill."

"Who's he?"

"He's the guy that won the hounds. Or his dog did. You should have seen his dog—looked kind of like an old Brillo pad. But a cute Brillo pad. It was something called an otter hound."

"And I should talk to the owner of the Brillo pad?"

"Yes. Because, after you snuck away with that woman, I heard someone say that if Mel Sweeten's dogs had been there, the Brillo pad never would have won."

"Aha. You think maybe this guy Dill killed Mel Sweeten so his Brillo pad could win the hound group at the dog show."

"It's a possibility. Isn't it?"

"Right. Okay, Jackie, I have to get back to work now. Listen, let me know if you make any more earth-shattering discoveries."

"Sure thing."

They hung up.

" 'Sylvia,' " muttered Jackie aloud, as she thumbed impatiently through her note cards on Harold Lloyd. "He calls her 'Sylvia.' "

At his desk at Palmer Central, Michael McGowan doodled on a note pad.

Last night he had interviewed Sylvia Brown at length. He was still trying to piece together his impressions. One thing you could be sure of, Sylvia Brown wasn't shy about trying to make an impression.

"And *eight, seven, six, five, four, three, two, one*," said Sylvia Brown. "Remember to breathe," she coached. "Now, take it down and *stretch* it out, good! *Eight, seven, six, five, four, three, two, one*."

Jackie, sweating and groaning her way through forty-five minutes of vigorous aerobics, wondered vaguely what "it" was. Whenever someone taught an exercise class, they told you to take *it* down, and stretch *it* out, or do a variety of other things to "it." In her experience, every aerobics and calisthenics teacher in the world talked about "it."

It was well that Jackie's mind was thus occupied, for the class was a strain. She realized with chagrin that it had been many months since she'd had any kind of serious exercise. This time, she vowed half seriously, she would stick with it. Sylvia Brown's was an early evening class—five-thirty— and the gym was just two blocks from home. It would be easy to get there two, three times a week, she fantasized— she could drop Peter over at Isaac Cook's house for an hour. Soon, Jackie vowed, she would be in really magnificent shape.

There was no question that Sylvia Brown gave you something to aim for. Her height alone would have made her impressive; but in her Day-Glo spandex suit, she looked less like Bathsheba than she did like some fierce Amazon, or a goddess out of Greek mythology. Like Diana the huntress, chaste and fair. Well, Sylvia was fair, anyway, reflected Jackie. There was no way Diana would have fallen for a guy like Mel Sweeten, not with Apollo around.

"Time for everyone's favorite: ab*dom*inals," Sylvia

Brown called to the class. The women dutifully hauled
out mats and began a punishing round of sit-ups. "And
crunch, and *up* and *up* and *up*! Come on, you can do
it," Sylvia urged, smiling at the class as she crunched.
Apparently Sylvia had muscles of steel. Like those steel
fibers that they made radial tires from. "Just sixteen
more!"

Jackie's stomach muscles protested fearsomely. This was
probably the punishment she deserved for sticking her nose
where it didn't belong. Also for those french fries, which
she had repented of already in Dick Buzone's office. *Never
again, never again,* she said to herself, crunching up. *No
more fries, ever again.*

When class was over, Jackie lay exhausted on her mat
and watched wearily to see what Sylvia Brown would do.
As Jackie had hoped, she headed for the women's locker
room. As soon as she recovered her strength, Jackie followed. She had come equipped with shampoo and towel,
for the sake of verisimilitude, but Sylvia apparently hadn't
worked out hard enough to need a shower. She had barely
raised a glimmer of perspiration. Jackie, feeling her age,
groaned inwardly.

"Great class," Jackie said brightly, hoping that nobody
would keep score of the lies she was telling. All in a
good cause.

"Thanks," replied Sylvia, somewhat vacantly. "You're
new to my class, aren't you?"

Jackie nodded. "Actually, my son and I just moved to
Palmer about six months ago. So we're sort of new to
everything around here."

"It's not a bad city. Working?" She spun the combination
of her locker.

"I teach film history at Rodgers." Jackie pulled off her
limp T-shirt and quickly donned an old turtleneck.

"Oh. Right around the corner." Sylvia slipped a pair of warm-up sweats over her spandex suit. "Like it?"

"Pretty much. I taught there a while ago, actually—then I got married and moved away. Now—well, I'm back again."

"Back in the saddle."

"More or less." Jackie struggled into her baggiest jeans. Honestly, it was terrible the way you could just let yourself go. Women built like Sylvia Brown didn't have this kind of problem. It wasn't fair—it was like Dick Buzone's hair. Jackie sucked in her stomach, trying not to be obvious. She would have to do something about it. Well, she *was* doing something about it, sort of. At least tonight.

"Listen," she began hopefully, when she had her blue jeans zipped up. "Um, I was talking to someone the other day who thought you might be able to help me."

Sylvia Brown looked at her swiftly. "Thought I could? Help you?"

"Yes—you see, my son Peter and I thought it might be kind of fun to enter our dog in a dog show—except that we don't know anything about it. Then someone told me that you do that professionally—take dogs to dog shows, that is. And I thought, 'What a coincidence!' because I had already decided to sign up for your aerobics class."

As Sylvia Brown listened, her expression changed from interest to wariness. "Who told you?"

"Huh?"

"I said, who told you about me?"

Jackie thought fast. For some reason, she was impelled to avoid the mention of Dick Buzone. "Just somebody I met on Sunday. I went down to the dog show at the armory. Some guy with a big black dog, who looked sort of like a poodle. The dog, I mean, not the guy."

Sylvia Brown swung her gym bag over her shoulder and

gave Jackie a long, thoughtful look. "Ralph Stevens?" she asked finally.

"*That's* the guy," Jackie exclaimed, stuffing her gym clothes into a tote bag. "I couldn't think of his name for the life of me."

"Huh." Sylvia Brown led the way out of the locker room and down a ramshackle staircase to the ground floor. "What kind of a dog do you have?"

"A German shepherd."

"A puppy?" They had reached the street and paused in front of the gym door. The early dark of the March night had settled in around them like a blanket. It was cold, and damp, and the street lamp in front of the entrance to the gym seemed to have something wrong with it. It hissed and buzzed, and flickered into a pale yellowish-gray life, only to die again, every few seconds.

Jackie was suddenly conscious of the sleeping strength of the other woman—of her height, and the power she had displayed in class. With a chill, Jackie wondered if she had made an enormous error in judgment.

Nobody knew she was here. Peter was at Isaac's house, but he had made that plan ages ago—the two were working on a history project together. Jake was at home, guarding the house. And Jackie hadn't been smart enough, or humble enough, to tell McGowan of her plan to see Sylvia Brown tonight.

Yet she knew that this woman could easily have pulled that collar tight around Mel Sweeten's neck. What was more, she knew a little bit about what kind of a woman she was—fairly ruthless, at a guess. The best that could be said was that she bad allowed herself to become involved with a married man. Nor had her approach to Michael McGowan, on Sunday at the armory, been lost on Jackie.

Jackie's blood ran cold. Did Sylvia Brown remember

seeing her at the armory on Sunday? Had she noticed the conspiratorial look that had passed between herself and Lieutenant McGowan?

Jackie forced herself to continue the conversation as normally as possible.

"A puppy? Oh—no. He's grown-up, all trained and very well behaved. He's ten, we think. More or less. Which way are you going?"

"Over to Chestnut Street." She looked at her watch. "Going to meet a friend. How about you?"

"Home—just a few blocks from here."

They began to walk together toward a working street-light. Jackie began to wonder if it was reasonable to be so suspicious of this woman. There could be another, more prosaic reason why Jackie wasn't taking a shine to Sylvia Brown. If she got home in one piece tonight, she'd have to examine her motives very carefully.

"For a show dog, you know, ten's kind of past it," said Sylvia Brown, her tone dismissive.

On the other hand, Jackie reflected, maybe the woman was just really and truly a jerk.

"Well, we don't expect him to win very many prizes, but I kind of thought it might be a good hobby for Peter."

"Your son?"

"Yep."

"How little is he?" Sylvia Brown's tone was not that of a woman with a fondness for children.

"He's ten too." Jackie took a deep breath. The air was freezing. She dug her hands deeper into her pockets and hunched up her shoulders. "I thought it might take his mind off of things, a little bit. There have been a lot of changes for him lately."

They had reached the corner, and stood there talking for a few more moments. "Thank you for asking, but I really don't know if I'll be keeping up the dog handling," said Sylvia. "I had a bad experience." She looked at Jackie sharply. "A good friend of mine, the person whose dogs I used to work with, was recently killed."

Jackie was taken aback. She hadn't anticipated that Sylvia Brown would open up to her in this way. "That must be very hard for you," she said lamely.

"Maybe you've heard about it," Sylvia went on, giving Jackie a sharp look.

"Um, could be. If you mean the man who was murdered at the Dog Academy, yes, I did read about it."

"He was a very good friend of mine," Sylvia said, as though to make sure Jackie understood. She looked at Jackie with something like appeal in her eyes. "I had worked with his dogs for a long time, so we knew each other very well. We talked to each other a lot, told each other things. And he was murdered, and I don't know why he was murdered, or who would want to kill him. I'm terrified."

Jackie was impressed. If this confidence was a put-on, it was excellently contrived. Of course she was scared—the mistress of the murdered man, to whom he had confided all his secrets, would naturally be frightened. Unless she knew herself, for some reason, to be safe. Unless, perhaps, she had done the murder herself.

"I don't blame you for being shocked and worried," said Jackie. "Last fall, someone in my department was murdered. I was shaken up for weeks afterward. I think I can understand how you feel."

"Can you?" Sylvia Brown lifted a well-kept eyebrow. "Maybe." She shrugged. "I think I'd better say no for now. But maybe I'll change my mind. Okay?"

"Sure," said Jackie. "Thanks a lot."

They parted.

Jackie, as she headed for Isaac Cook's house to collect

Peter, wondered if all of her speculation was foolish. Sylvia Brown seemed perfectly nice, for an adulteress. If she even was an adulteress. Amy, after all, had no proof that this was the person Mel had been involved with. And even if it had been Sylvia Brown, he had probably been a bum husband to start with. Amy was certainly better off with him gone.

For just a moment, thinking about marriages and mistresses, Jackie was swept with an unaccustomed bitterness over the failure of her own marriage. For an instant, Jackie felt that she would give anything to be once more in the happy first years of her marriage to Cooper, before his selfish indulgence had poisoned everything that the two of them had built together.

The sensation lasted only a moment, however. Jackie was a practical woman, and she knew that dwelling on such idle wishes would be the road to collapse. So she firmly redirected her thoughts. She and Peter had much to be grateful for in their new life—she especially, now that she was freed from the confines of a life that had not suited her. The bitterness passed, and Jackie was left feeling merely a sort of mild contempt for Sylvia Brown, whom she had privately labeled a home-wrecker.

But that was idiotic, she realized, shaking her head. Amy Sweeten hadn't made a home for herself and her husband. She had merely lodged at the Dog Academy, just another domestic animal, like the boarder dogs or the champion basset hounds, Fred and Karen. Except that, unlike Fred and Karen, Amy hadn't even loved Mel—on the contrary, she was glad that he was dead.

Jackie decided that Amy's was a funny attitude, no matter how you looked at it.

On the other hand, what on earth had Sylvia Brown seen in Mel Sweeten? By all accounts, he had thought about nothing but dogs, dog shows, breeding and selling dogs, training dogs, and just being around dogs. Whereas Jackie was pretty certain that Sylvia Brown had other interests.

CHAPTER 13

On Thursday morning, in his office at Palmer Central, Michael McGowan was refining the target of the police investigation into the murder of Mel Sweeten. He had been unconvinced by Jackie's talk of the high pitch of emotions among the dog-show crowd, and he had done some serious spadework on a more prosaic level. Finally, this morning, he had unearthed something that looked like a lead. The information was contained in a stack of impenetrable money-market investment reports, now piled high on his desk.

He looked again at the trades, and made careful notes. Mel Sweeten had a nephew, a young man of about twenty-six, by the name of Ned Whiting. He had recently gone to work at Nash Brothers, the most respected investment firm in Palmer. The young stockbroker had been mentioned in Sweeten's will as one of the principal beneficiaries of the victim's estate, which turned out to have been quite large. At least it seemed large to McGowan, who didn't really understand how it was possible to make a million dollars running a dog kennel and going to dog shows. But such was life. And there it was—Mel Sweeten had been a millionaire.

The term "millionaire" nowadays was rather discounted;

there were plenty of millionaires who bore little resemblance to the top-hatted tycoon on the Monopoly box. But you couldn't argue with inheritance as a motive to murder. What was more, Ned Whiting had managed his uncle's investment portfolio, which Nash Brothers had valued on the last day of December at about three hundred thousand dollars. It was a nice chunk of change for a young man to be managing on his own.

At last, McGowan and his forces had something a little more solid to go on. He had never wanted to believe that the mysterious other woman and her displaced nightgown were all that important to the murder investigation.

Two days earlier, McGowan had met briefly with Whiting to talk about the inheritance. Now, after looking quickly through the money-market records, he decided it was time to interview the young broker again. But first he needed some background. He picked up the phone and called an old classmate from high school days, Johnny Shaw, who was now a managing partner at Nash Brothers.

When the two old friends had finished discussing the bleak hopes of the Palmer basketball team for the present season, McGowan came to the point. "You have a young man there by the name of Whiting," he said finally.

"I didn't really think you were calling to talk basketball," said Shaw, relief in his tone. "I'm glad you called. I'd been wondering if I ought to call you, in view of the large amount of money we were managing for that Sweeten character."

McGowan's interest stirred. "Has anyone there looked over the portfolio?"

"I did. Shortly after the trading for it was suspended."

"And?"

"And I didn't like what I saw."

"Glad to hear that. Now, explain. This stuff is gibberish to me, you know."

"Right. Well, the file is incomplete, for one thing. There appear to be confirmation slips missing for certain trades; their absence may or may not indicate some sort of malfeasance. The numbers for the account don't really add up, either. But it's more than likely to be just sloppiness. He's a sloppy kid, that Whiting. And the account was losing money. Ned Whiting was picking bad buys."

Shaw went on, enumerating some of the transactions recorded in the file. More than half of them had been substantial losses. McGowan listened in silence as Shaw went over some of the trades.

"Does the record mean anything?" the detective asked at last.

"To me, yes, of course. It means that Whiting doesn't have any investment sense."

"Anything besides that?"

"Not technically, no. But I don't understand why the numbers don't add up. It almost looks as though there were some extra funds coming in, which is not the way it usually works in cases of embezzlement. If that's what you're thinking about."

"We have to consider every angle," said McGowan.

"Well, one thing you can be sure of. If this is more than just sloppiness, we would have caught it quickly enough— we have an internal system in place, just in case. He would have been found out by the end of the month, at the latest. Which is why I'm inclined to think he was just being lazy, not following through with the paperwork."

"On the other hand," said McGowan, his voice heavy with satisfaction, "maybe he was robbing his uncle blind."

"I suppose there's always that possibility," Shaw agreed. "And if so, Nash Brothers will have to face it squarely. Let me know if there's anything else you need."

"Will do," said McGowan.

An hour later, Ned Whiting sat smoothly in one of the two hard wooden chairs in McGowan's office. He had come quickly from his office when McGowan phoned, professing himself happy to be of service to the police; he had maintained his cool as McGowan questioned him closely about Mel Sweeten's portfolio.

Now he leaned his lanky body easily back in the chair and regarded McGowan with a challenging stare. The smooth planes of his face seemed to gleam in the fluorescent light; his dark hair, which was on the long side, had an almost indigo cast to it. His eyebrows were heavy and thick, a dark line dividing his face. He looked every inch a successful young stockbroker—with his boldly striped but still conservative shirt, bright red suspenders, and four-hundred-dollar shoes. He had arrived in a bright red Porsche convertible, which was now parked outside in the lot, next to McGowan's ten-year-old Dodge station wagon. Straight or bent, Ned Whiting was doing all right for himself.

"Look, Lieutenant," the young man said, "I agree that my uncle's portfolio might have been better managed. But I don't see why that's any of your business, frankly."

"Anything and everything is my business, if I want it to be," said McGowan. "I understand that there are confirmation slips missing from the file. Which either signifies that you were neglecting your fiduciary duty, or that you were acting without your uncle's approval."

"Uncle Mel didn't know the first thing about investing. He only knew about dogs. So his approval wouldn't have been meaningful, for my purposes."

"That's not relevant. I've been through some records that he kept at his house and compared those records to the file." He tapped the large stack of computer printouts. "There were trades that he apparently asked you to make, for which there are no confirmation slips." Johnny Shaw had explained that the confirmation slips were the firm's way of making certain that a client knew exactly what was happening to his money. The absence of such records could mean that Whiting had been pocketing the investment money that came in to his account at Nash. "That suggests to me the possibility that you were playing fast and loose with his money."

"No way," protested Whiting. "There's just no way I would have tried something like that. I would have been caught within the week. At Nash Brothers we have all kinds of systems in place to detect that kind of thing."

"Suppose you tell me, then, about the missing confirmation slips."

"They're not 'missing'—I just never got around to sorting through things and getting the hard-copy file up-to-date. The computer records will show the trades, and that's all that counts, really."

"Except for the fact that you didn't tell your uncle what you were doing with his money."

"We've been through this, Lieutenant." A supercilious smile flitted across Whiting's pudgy lips, and he leaned forward with a patient look on his face. "There is absolutely no way for you to demonstrate that my uncle didn't know, so I suggest you abandon this line. Either that, or take my word for it."

"And then," McGowan went on, "there's always the possibility that your uncle discovered that you had been defying him. He called you, I imagine, to talk about the situation. You made an appointment to see him after the meeting that was already scheduled to take place at his house that night. At about nine o'clock, you headed over to the Dog Academy and solved the problem. It didn't take long at all, really. You solved your problem, and you got the cash you wanted. Maybe you even needed the cash."

"That's ridiculous."

"I'm not so sure. Let's hear where you were the night that your uncle was killed."

"We have been through this a hundred times. Right after work, I went to Charlie's Place with some of the other brokers. We hung out there for a few hours, drank a lot of beer, and then about nine-thirty I left. I didn't feel like going home, so I decided to go to the movies. The Senator Theater is on my way home, so I stopped in for the ten o'clock show of *Thelma and Louise*. By myself."

"Do you often go to movies alone?"

"Hardly ever," said Whiting with a grin. "But that's not the kind of movie you take your girlfriend to, Lieutenant. Not unless you want to give her a bad idea about men."

"All right. What did you do after the movie was over?"

"I went home. You can ask the doorman in my apartment building."

They went over and over the same ground. Finally, McGowan decided that he would do better if he gave the suspect a rest. Ned Whiting was an extremely cocky young man; if he thought he had the police fooled, he might trip himself up.

McGowan kept Whiting for another half an hour or so, then finally dismissed him. He was pretty sure he had his man. And now that he had someone in his sights, McGowan was prepared to play a patient waiting game. Experience had taught him that this was the soundest approach.

CHAPTER 14

At six o'clock that evening, having accepted Cosmo Gordon's invitation to meet for a beer at the Juniper Tavern, Michael McGowan was feeling satisfied. He was busy filling his colleague in on the details of his interview with Ned Whiting and his conversation with Johnny Shaw.

The Juniper Tavern was the kind of spot where you could be sure of cold beer and cold beer mugs, of hamburgers and french fries done to your liking, and of waitresses and bartenders who remembered your name. The Juniper was cozy, and usually full in the evenings. The tables and booths were made of solid wood, and the long bar that ran half the length of the main room was a century old, made of dark mahogany with well-shined brass detailing and a long mirror behind it, against the wall, framed in the same dark mahogany, but intricately carved. Gordon and McGowan were seated far in the back, in the last booth on the right, which was their usual spot when they could get it. It afforded the privacy that their conversations often demanded.

"Nephew," said McGowan, reaching for a french fry and dunking it in ketchup. "It's perfect. He's twenty-six, living it up, a broker at Nash Brothers. According to a credit check we ran this afternoon, he's pretty deeply in debt. Got a car worth about fifty grand, and a half-paid-for condo, and shoes that would cost me a week's pay, and zippo in the bank."

"So he's like the rest of his generation," said Gordon. "That doesn't make him a killer."

"He had a big-time motive," replied McGowan.

"You think?" asked Gordon. "Did he stand to inherit?"

"A big chunk of cash—close to half a million."

Gordon whistled. "There's your motive, anyway."

"Not only that. He was managing the portfolio for Nash Brothers, but the records appear to indicate that he was stealing from his uncle. John Shaw says the internal system would have caught him by the end of the month."

"Doesn't sound like a bright fellow."

"Top of his class, obviously," concurred McGowan. "So the beer's on me. We're well on our way to wrapping that one up. What's new on your end?"

Gordon looked uncomfortable. "Something has happened. I feel kind of silly, but I thought I'd talk to you about it. If it's nothing to worry about, tell me, and I'll just forget all about it."

"What on earth are you talking about?"

"This." Gordon reached for his briefcase, which was sitting on the bench beside him, and opened it. Carefully, he withdrew a clear plastic envelope, which he laid on the table.

Inside was another envelope, ordinary letter size, with Gordon's name and address typed on the front.

McGowan carefully turned the plastic envelope over. The other side of the inner envelope was blank.

"Nice," said McGowan. "Got a sweetheart you haven't told Nancy about?"

"Right," said Gordon, evidently in no mood to joke. He reached into the briefcase and brought out a larger plastic envelope. This one contained a letter, typewritten, on ordinary bond. McGowan could see at a glance that it would be hopeless to try to trace the paper and the typewriter. He reached for the plastic envelope and held it carefully.

Dear Dr. Gordon,
    We know that you had a meeting with an old friend of yours. It's important to us to know what your friend said to you. We can't ask him, so we'll have to ask you, at a time and place of our choosing.
    Be sure to keep yourself available.

"Nice one," said McGowan, putting it down gently on the table.

"You think it's for real?" Gordon sounded relieved. Better to face actual danger than to make yourself ridiculous by falling for some schoolboy hoax.

"Got to be." McGowan shook his head. "I guess old Matt knew what he was talking about."

"You think they're talking about Dugan? About the night he came to see us, just before he was killed."

"Got to be," replied McGowan. "Somebody wants to meet with you, find out what you know."

Gordon looked abashed. "I could kill myself, really, for not listening to Matt more carefully that night. But he was rambling. You don't know the way he had begun to just go on and on and on. He'd come up real close to you, and look at you with these sad blue eyes of his that could hardly focus, and all I could ever think about was how sad it all was. He used to be a great cop. Great."

Gordon downed his beer and signaled the waitress for two more. "We've gotta get to the bottom of this, Mike. I owe it to my old buddy."

"Right you are." McGowan looked at the anonymous letter again. "You'd better let forensics take a look."

"Oh, I will, don't worry. I'll drop it by the lab on my way home tonight. I just didn't want to make a fool of myself."

"Nope. God forbid you should make a fool of yourself."

Not far from the Juniper Tavern, in an up-scale bistro that was the habitual hangout of Palmer's advertising professionals, designers, and graphic artists, another tête-à-tête was taking place.

"I told you, Dick, I'm sick and tired of all of this," said Sylvia Brown. She ran a hand through her long blond hair. Her face, reflected in a long mirror behind a chrome-and-marble bar, looked haggard. She was not a very good advertisement, at this moment, for the virtues of aerobic exercise. But perhaps that was because she hadn't slept peacefully in over a week.

Dick Buzone snickered and lifted his glass, glancing casually at his reflection in the mirror as he sipped at a very dry martini. "And I told you, my dear, that you will do what I say."

His voice, ordinarily thin and reedy, held an unaccustomed hint of a threat this afternoon.

"Why?" asked Sylvia defiantly. "I went out on a limb for you. In a big way. And so far, there's nothing to show for it." She stared at him defiantly.

Buzone smirked, his thin lips wriggling like little flesh-toned caterpillars. "Patience, my dear. Anything worth having is worth waiting for. That's what I tell all those silly women who want me to give their dogs blue ribbons. Patience will bring you rewards." He sipped gently at his drink.

"You and your famous patience." She took a hearty swig of her club soda. "If you ask me, I think that detective is on to something."

"Why?"

"He keeps calling me in to police headquarters for these long interviews." She rolled her eyes. "I'm not sure exactly what he's after, what he wants. But he's definitely after something."

"Maybe he just wants to date you." Buzone smiled faintly, as though he had made a joke. He apparently thought that the idea of anyone's wanting to date Sylvia Brown was absurd.

"I think I know the difference, Dick," said Sylvia with venom. "God knows I've had enough experience."

"Get next to him. Figure out if he knows anything. Or talk to that nosy broad, his girlfriend." It was an order. Buzone smacked his thin little lips together and gave his reflection an approving glance. He enjoyed giving orders.

"What girlfriend?" Sylvia Brown sounded annoyed.

"The one I sent to see you. Dark hair, teaches film history at Rodgers."

"Jackie Walsh? You sent her to see me?"

Buzone shrugged. "She came to me with some cock-and-bull story about her dog, or her son's dog. I took her money and told her to hire you. Find out why she came to see me."

"Forget it."

Buzone looked sharply at Sylvia. "What do you mean by that?"

"I mean forget it. From now on you can count me out. My classes at the gym are doing really well, and I don't want to hang around dog shows for the rest of my life. So let's just call it quits. We're about even."

"No, my dear. You don't quit until I tell you to." Buzone

had reached out and grabbed one of Sylvia's wrists. He began to twist.

"Let go of me, you creep," said Sylvia. She caught the bartender's eye. He came striding swiftly over.

"Everything okay, ma'am?" he asked with a practiced look at Buzone.

"No. Everything is not okay. This man is trying to molest me, and it's not the first time. I'd like you to call the police."

The color drained from Buzone's face. "You little—"

"I think you'd better leave, sir," said the bartender, who had seen this kind of thing before.

"Don't pay the slightest attention to her," said Buzone, recovering his icy composure. "She's crazy. Just got out of treatment for severe paranoia."

"Right, and you're Doctor Jekyll," retorted Sylvia. "If you come near me again, I swear I'll call the cops." She gathered up her gym bag and her pocketbook and put on her coat. Then, without pausing even to look at Buzone, she stormed out into the cold March air.

Buzone gave the bartender a knowing look. "She can't help herself," said Buzone, man-to-man. "She's in love."

CHAPTER 15

On Thursday afternoon at lunchtime, Jackie ran into Amy Sweeten in the faculty cafeteria. She hadn't seen the young widow since the day they'd talked at Amy's house, almost a week ago; Amy looked better, more lively, but she was still as pale as ashes. She asked Jackie to share a table with her in the corner.

"Are you all right?" asked Jackie, sure this was a necessary question. Amy Sweeten looked anything but all right.

"I'm fine," came the response. Amy's voice was surprisingly clear and strong. "Just tired of talking to policemen all the time."

"I can imagine," responded Jackie sympathetically. "Have you heard about any progress on the case?"

Amy Sweeten shrugged her thin little shoulders. "I guess they're trying everything they can think of. One of them came out to the house last night and got all of our financial records for the last six months." Amy grinned slightly. "Including Mel's credit-card slips, and all of his motel bills."

"Oh." Jackie took a thoughtful bite of her tuna-fish sandwich. "You think they're looking at that angle still?"

"How should I know?" Amy sounded as though she didn't care. "All I know is that they never seem to leave me alone. I wish they would. I'm ready to get on with my life."

Amy's way of talking unnerved Jackie. Mel Sweeten had been dead less than two weeks, and already his widow was bored with the murder investigation. How would she feel if they kept it up for months? Jackie shook her head. Art historians were supposed to understand that the process of inquiry could be lengthy. Maybe Amy didn't have the patience for scholarship.

"At least," said Amy, sounding just a bit affronted, "they could investigate that woman."

"Which woman?" asked Jackie, sure of the answer.

"The one he was having the affair with. The one who left her nightgown in the hotel."

"Amy, are you *sure* that Mel was having an affair with her?"

"Of course I am. He went away almost every weekend with her, to one of those stupid dog shows. I think she's the one that did it. Don't you?"

"How should I know?"

"Have you seen her?"

Jackie considered briefly whether or not to lie. This conversation was getting on her nerves; Amy Sweeten had a dull, childlike flatness to her voice that was most annoying. On the other hand, there wasn't really any reason to hold back the whole truth.

"I did see her, actually. I went to the dog show last Sunday, and she was there."

"You *did*? You went to the dog show to look at her, didn't you? Isn't she awful?"

"I wouldn't call her awful." Jackie felt a sudden urge to rush to Sylvia Brown's defense. She wasn't close enough to Amy to feel otherwise.

"She *is* awful. All you have to do is look at her."

Jackie wanted to change the subject. "What about the business?"

"Huh?"

"The Dog Academy. What's going to happen to it?"

Amy Sweeten shrugged her tiny shoulders. "Tom Mann resigned. There weren't any dogs there, anyway. Not much business. Now all I have to do is figure out about Fred and Karen. You want some basset hounds?"

Jackie shook her head. She had thought Fred and Karen were very lovable-looking, but she was sure there were plenty of professionals who might be interested in them. She expressed the idea to Amy.

"Oh, there are. My phone never stops ringing, and they're all calling about the dogs. They all ask me, 'How are they coping?' As if I could possibly know how a basset hound feels. It's idiotic. They don't give a damn about how *I* feel. They're just like Mel."

"Oh!" said Jackie. She hadn't thought about it, but it must be galling to have your dead husband's friends all inquiring about the emotional state of the dogs. "Is there anyone in particular they might go to?"

"Well, there's a woman who wants them, but she and Mel hated each other, so I don't know."

"She's a dog-show type?" asked Jackie, feeling a prickle of curiosity.

"Yeah. She raises beagles, but that's almost the same."

"The beagle lady," murmured Jackie. "I think I saw her at the dog show. Her name is Thalia Gilmore."

"That's the one," replied Amy, nodding. "Thalia Gilmore. Mel couldn't stand her. She banned him from some club or something. They had one of those feuds about nothing that go on and on for years."

"I'm surprised she wants Mel's dogs," said Jackie.

"I'm not. Everyone knows they're the best bassets. In

fact, that Gilmore woman bought one of Karen's puppies, a couple of years ago, but it turned out to be a dud, never won any ribbons."

"But she's willing to try again?"

"I guess so. She offered me a thousand dollars for the two of them. What should I do? Should I take it?"

Jackie thought that Amy should do anything that would keep the poor bassets from languishing any longer in their kennel, so she was on the verge of urging Amy to accept the offer. A thousand dollars seemed like a lot of money for two dogs; and the feud obviously didn't extend to the dogs.

On the other hand, perhaps Thalia Gilmore was pulling a fast one on Amy—to get back at Mel, or to exact some other kind of weird satisfaction. Or just to get champion dogs at bargain-basement prices. It might be smart to ask around.

"I'll tell you what," she responded at last. "Why don't I look into the question for you? I'll talk to some of these dog people that I've met and find out what the going price would be for two champions like Fred and Karen. Okay?"

"That would be great," replied Amy flatly.

Jackie turned the conversation to other topics—Rodgers University was going to the regional championships in basketball, and everyone, even art historians and other-worldly professors of astrophysics, were breathless with anticipation. So the lunch ended on an upbeat note, but when Jackie returned to her office she thought long and hard.

It occurred to her that the person who most deserved those two dogs was Sylvia Brown. She had been the one, after all, who had worked with them over and over again, helping to bring them to the top. Amy, of course, would probably not stand for it. But if Sylvia Brown wasn't a murderer, she really did seem to be the logical person to take the dogs. After fifteen minutes Jackie still hadn't thought of a solution, short of using herself as a front should Sylvia want to buy the dogs. And that seemed like drastic cloak-and-dagger stuff. Better, perhaps, not to stir the pot. Better to let sleeping dogs lie.

On the other hand, she had every intention of filling Michael McGowan in on the bit of gossip that Amy had passed along. Were the police aware that Mel Sweeten and Thalia Gilmore were enemies?

When she got home that evening, Jackie's course was made smoother by an unexpected telephone call from Sylvia Brown. She had changed her mind, she told Jackie, and would like to take Jake to the obedience trials on Saturday morning. If Jackie and Peter were still interested?

Jackie, intrigued, accepted. She wondered what on earth had prompted Sylvia's change of heart. She would just have to wait until Saturday—but she was determined to find out.

CHAPTER 16

On Friday afternoon, after a long week, Jackie decided to give Michael McGowan a call. She had to admit to herself that she was just the tiniest bit annoyed with him— he seemed to have been neglecting her of late. He was always happy to invite himself for dinner when he wanted something—when he wanted to borrow Jake for his investigation, for instance—but in between those exigencies he rarely called or came by. Jackie had begun to wonder if he were a fair-weather friend. Or if maybe there were some other, more personal reason why he was keeping her at arm's length from the investigation.

Jackie was looking forward to Saturday. Mel Sweeten's murder still intrigued her, and the obedience competition would give her a much-needed change of pace. In her film history class, they had spent the entire week on the work of Jean-Luc Godard, whom Jackie privately considered a bore and an impostor. But the French filmmaker's work was influential and famous, of that there could be little doubt. So Jackie had forced herself to sit through a screening of *Weekend,* and generously forbore to tell her class that she found Godard's situations contrived and sententious. A few in the class had reached the same conclusion on their own, which had gladdened Jackie's heart, but after giving two hour-long lectures on the Frenchman, she desperately needed to think about something practical, like murder.

Shortly before suppertime, she dialed McGowan's number. He professed himself glad to hear from her, but she wasn't certain. There was an edge to his voice.

"I heard something interesting from Amy Sweeten," she told him.

"Oh, yeah?" McGowan sounded busy, harassed. "What's that?"

"That her husband had an enemy."

"We know that, Jackie. He got himself murdered."

"Michael, please don't be condescending. I mean there was a person that he was feuding with."

"Tell me."

"A woman who breeds beagles. I told you about her—I saw her at the dog show. She's the one that was complaining about the article in that dog newsletter."

"Oh, Thalia Gilmore. Right. Well, we're not really looking into that angle anymore. But thanks for the information. I'll file it, just in case."

Jackie was stung. "But, Michael," she protested, "you're the one that wanted to borrow Jake and go around to dog shows. Now I'm doing all this work for you, and you just brush me off."

McGowan's reticence seemed like treason. She had been such a willing helper when he asked. She had volunteered not only the services of her dog, but also her own time. And now he was acting as though she were some kind of loony. Worse, he was acting as though he were trying to keep her at a distance. Personally. As if she had ever encouraged him!

Quite suddenly, Jackie made up her mind. She was going to beat him to the punch. She would find out who had killed Mel Sweeten.

But she decided to play it fair, and play it safe. She didn't want another moment of panic like the one she'd experienced the other night, all alone in the darkened road with Sylvia Brown. There was no evidence, so far, that the woman was not a killer.

"Well, anyway, Michael, I don't mind if you're not interested, but I'll tell you anyway. First about Thalia Gilmore, and then about Sylvia Brown. I don't want you telling me that I didn't fill you in, in case I come up with the answer before you do."

McGowan laughed. "Okay, Jackie. Listen. Don't be mad at me, okay? If I could tell you everything that's going on at this end, I would. You just have to trust me on this. Detective work has a certain amount of confidentiality to it—and that's for your safety as much as anything else. But I will tell you that I'm working on a very strong lead, one that has nothing to do with dogs or dog shows or someone being jealous of someone else's dog, or anything remotely like that. Okay?"

"But what about Thalia Gilmore?"

"I've talked to her. She admitted that she had reason to hate Mel Sweeten, but she had hated him for years. Besides, her son vouches for her. He lives with her."

"Oh, great."

"I know what you mean. But unless we can impeach her alibi, we'll have to swallow it. Dick Buzone, the man that you love to hate, says that the executive committee ended the meeting at about eight-fifteen. He remembers because he was going to meet a friend, and he was a few minutes late."

"I suppose his friend alibis him too."

"Sure. They went to a party. A big, noisy party at the new club that was opening downtown. A charity benefit, or something, with all the local advertising bigwigs. It was the kind of thing where you don't see your date for hours."

"So he *could* have done it."

"So could you or I, if you think like that. Jackie, trust me on this. There is more to this murder than just dogs and dog shows. Okay?"

"If you say so." Jackie was unconvinced. She wanted to talk to Thalia Gilmore, face-to-face. She was already convinced that Dick Buzone could murder thirty people without giving it a thought, but it would have to profit him greatly. He struck her as the kind of person who never did anything without the assurance of great personal gain.

"Oh, by the way, Michael. There's one other thing I wondered about. About Buzone."

"What's that?"

"Well, he just doesn't seem to be the type of guy who would get involved in a nonprofit thing like dog shows. Plus, I don't think he really likes dogs very much. If I were a dog, I wouldn't go near him. He just doesn't have that doggy personality, if you know what I mean."

"I do," replied McGowan. "He's more like a flounder."

"Not a flounder," said Jackie with spirit. "He's an eel. An eel with hair."

"So he is."

"Right. And maybe there's some dirt on him somewhere."

"You can find dirt on anyone, if you look hard enough. As our political process seems to prove every election year."

"Yes, but—"

"Tell you what," said McGowan, his voice pacifying. He wanted to make Jackie feel better about being left out of the investigation. "Try to dig up some dirt on Buzone from the dog people you see tomorrow. And if there's anything useful for the investigation, I'll fill you in completely. Okay?"

"It's a deal," Jackie answered, somewhat mollified.

CHAPTER 17

Thus on the following Saturday morning, Jackie, Peter, Isaac Cook, Jake, and Sylvia Brown were all piled into Jackie's Jeep, headed for Wardville High School, whose gymnasium and playing fields today would be the setting for the Greater Palmer Canine Obedience Competition.

Peter was thoroughly pleased. At last he'd have a chance to show the world how truly great and impressive a dog Jake was. He and Isaac knew, for a fact, that Jake would win every prize in the book. He was the best-trained dog in the world.

Last night, as the two boys talked on the phone to make arrangements, Isaac had expressed skepticism. He was concerned that "some lady" was going to be putting Jake through his paces. But Peter, having learned of Sylvia's credentials, was quick to put his friend's mind to rest. "It'll be cake for Jake, and we know it," he said. "Jake knows what he knows. The lady doesn't matter."

"Yeah, but what if she says something like 'Get him, Jake'? Remember what happened to my sweater?" Isaac was referring to a training session that he and Peter had had with Jake last fall. That was the day when the boys discovered the range and depth of Jake's training. It had been an aweseome experience. Jake's power wasn't something to be trifled with.

"Look," Peter had explained patiently. "She's a dog trainer. She won't do anything stupid like that."

Thus encouraged, Isaac had agreed to come along and be part of Jake's cheering section.

Now as the group headed out toward the school, Sylvia Brown was offering Jackie an explanation for her change of heart. "I got to thinking about it, you know—how I told you that since my friend had died I wasn't sure about keeping up with the dog-handling routine. But I figured that that attitude wasn't really in the right spirit. I mean, Mel wouldn't want me to give up. I know he wouldn't."

"Probably not," concurred Jackie.

"Besides, I've been working with his dogs for a really long time, and I figure that branching out is going to be tough for me. Emotionally, and also in the show ring. You get to know one breed pretty well, but then you're kind of stuck if someone asks you to take charge of another breed. Different temperaments, and different things that the judges look for. There's a lot of work in bringing a dog all the way to best of breed in a show; and to finish him you really have to know him."

"I can imagine," said Jackie, who hadn't previously considered the problem. She conjured up an image of the little white poodle, Serena, that she had seen at the dog show last Sunday. Certainly that dog had a different temperament— that dog had been all nerves. Undoubtedly you would have to know what you were getting into, to successfully handle a dog like that one. Jackie guessed that being a dog handler had its subtleties, much like any other profession. "What made you choose basset hounds in the first place?"

"Oh, I've always loved them. At first for their looks— they're so low, and long, and have such silky ears, and their paws are so adorable. But once you start to work with a breed, you find more to like in it than just its cuteness. Bassets are sturdy companions, true blue. I think that's why I like them so much."

There was a traffic jam outside the entrance to Wardville High; the Obedience Competition had apparently drawn a huge crowd. Peter and Isaac took off to look around, while Sylvia put Jake on his lead and went over to the area where the competitors were waiting. To Jackie fell the thankless task of waiting in line at the registration table. She watched her son and his friend as they nudged each other, laughing excitedly, and moved in for a closer look at some of the dogs. Jackie felt real happiness. For Peter, the transition from suburban life to city life had been easy—but a lot of that had to do with Isaac. The boys were such good friends. And of course, Jake had been a big part of it too. Jackie felt quite sure that Jake would win all the prizes, just as Peter had predicted.

As Jackie waited to fill in a card for Jake, she considered what Sylvia Brown had said in the car. Jackie didn't really believe that Sylvia had changed her mind out of fidelity to Mel Sweeten's memory; on the other hand, the woman's reasons for liking basset hounds had sounded, to her, like the truth. It seemed likely to Jackie that something had happened on Wednesday or Thursday to prompt Sylvia's call. She wanted to find out what it was.

The day was quite chilly, but Jackie had brought two large red-and-black checked blankets and several thermoses full of hot chocolate. As she and the boys found a good spot on one of the old benches along the side of the soccer field, there was great promise in the air.

The obedience competition was, to Jackie's mind, more of what a dog show should be all about—it looked like fun. There were fewer competitors, and some of them, like Jake himself, looked a little bit the worse for wear, in spite of the efforts that their owners and handlers were making to groom them for the occasion. But all the dogs, and the people as well, looked positively thrilled to be there. The school's grounds afforded plenty of room for wandering around and exploring, and the competitors' area, from what Jackie could tell, seemed to lack the ominous tension that she had sensed last Sunday at the armory.

Sylvia Brown had explained to them that today's event wasn't an important competition—just a preliminary heat, more of an informal get-together of dog lovers. The place was crowded with contestants and owners; only about twenty-five of the best dogs would be invited to compete in the formal competition two weeks from now.

The result was a carnival atmosphere. Off in a far corner of the large field, some teenagers had established their own competition for Frisbee-catching. At the opposite end, near the back of the gymnasium, a group of small children and their dogs seemed to be playing a canine version of "Duck, Duck, Goose." Jackie felt delighted—she loved to see dogs at play.

Sylvia had taken Jake off to do a few warm-ups with him before entering the competitors' area. The boys had gone off to watch the Frisbee-fetching competition, and Jackie decided to take a look around.

She wandered around among the crowd, slowly making her way toward a small table where coffee and hot chocolate were sold. A few of the faces were familiar to her from Sunday's outing at the armory. One of them was Thalia Gilmore, the beagle lady, hugely attired in a thick woolen suit of a color somewhere between mustard and puce. As she pushed through a knot of people, she reminded Jackie of a magnificent snowplow, or perhaps an icebreaker ship. She moved steadily forward with huge but stately calm, nodding this way and that, and the people parted before her.

Thalia Gilmore was accompanied today not by the spright-ly Clematis, who had competed on Sunday at the armory, but by a slightly misshapen liver-and-white basset hound. The dog was indisputably seedy and inclined to bay loudly and long, ignoring all orders to be quiet. The dog seemed to be the only living creature who didn't bow to Thalia Gilmore's will.

Jackie thought about the woman's offer to buy Fred and Karen from Amy Sweeten. This dog must be the "dud" that Amy had mentioned. He certainly didn't look like a show-stopper, that was for certain. But perhaps he had hidden virtues in the area of obedience skills.

Before long Jackie spotted Dick Buzone. Undoubtedly, as president of the local dog club, he had to put in an appearance at every meet. She watched as he approached Sylvia, who seemed bent on ignoring him. He said a few words to her, but she kept her back turned to him. Jackie was struck by something in the attitude of the two of them; there was an unmistakable familiarity in the way that Sylvia snubbed Buzone. It was easy to see.

Before long, the crowd seemed to come to attention. The competition was about to get under way, and Jackie and the boys took their seats. A large, red-faced man in a tweed suit and large tweed hat picked up a megaphone and began to speak to the crowd.

"Ladies and gentlemen, and contestants. Your attention please." The talk of the crowd lowered to a murmur, per-mitting the voices of the contestants to be heard, variously barking, yelping, and baying. Jackie thought she could pick out the voice of Thalia Gilmore's basset above all the rest of the noise.

"Please, ladies and gentlemen, ask your four-legged friends to be quiet."

Giggling and joking, Jackie and the boys settled into their seats. The competition was called to order, and one by one, dog after dog was put through his paces. The dogs heeled, they sat, they lay down, and they stayed; they bounded from one corner of the show area to another, and they walked sedately back. The retrievers were called upon to fetch things; others were required to stay quite still and ignore tantalizing objects, such as frankfurters, that were placed nearby.

Some of the dogs were real show-offs, but others seemed to take it all in stride. There were one or two excellent performances by golden retrievers, and a dog with no recognizable bloodlines came close to turning in a perfect performance. Thalia Gilmore's basset was as intractable as a goat, prompting great gusts of laughter from the crowd. Poor Thalia herself looked mortified, but the dog seemed to be utterly impervious to the amused scorn of the onlookers.

Jake's turn finally came. Sylvia, who had taken off a baggy sweatsuit to reveal a colorful spandex aerobics costume, led him into the center of the ring. It was hard to say who had more stage presence at that precise instant: Sylvia Brown certainly knew how to get the attention of the crowd, but Jake seemed, for the moment, a born performer. Jackie thought of Rin-Tin-Tin, and smiled. Peter and Isaac were mesmerized; there was no dog on earth like him. The others, good as they had been, seemed like beginners in comparison. They were out of his league.

"Isn't he great, Mom? Isn't he great?"

"Absolutely the best, Petey," said Jackie with real pride in her voice.

"I think Stella could do that," said Isaac, halfheartedly. Stella was one of his dogs. A huge, friendly thing with a coat that looked like a cinnamon bagel, she was part plott hound (Isaac thought) and part mystery dog.

Jake had golden assurance, and he walked with a surefooted and dignified tread. With silent grace he anticipated the orders that the judges called for, and he responded to Sylvia's hands and voice as though he had known her all his life. The audience grew a little quieter in appreciation as Jake unfailingly carried out every command given him. There was never a moment's hesitation; he had done it all so many times before.

He would win, hands down. There was no question of that.

After Jake had had his turn, Jackie and the boys got up to wander around again. Jackie headed over to where Thalia Gilmore, her face red, was trying to coax her basset hound into the back of her station wagon. The dog did not want to make the jump. He looked firmly at his mistress and sat down heavily.

Jackie, with a smile for Thalia Gilmore, stooped down to get a better look at the dog. Imperfect as he was, the basset was nonetheless adorable. She offered this opinion to his owner.

"Adorable. Yes, I suppose he might appear so to the uninitiated," was the stony reply. "Perhaps you'd care to take him home. If so, be my guest. He's all yours."

Jackie laughed. "We have one dog already," she answered easily. "And I think one's enough for now. But surely you don't want to give him away?"

"Don't I?" retorted Thalia Gilmore huffily. "Just look at him. He was supposed to come from champion stock."

"You think he didn't?"

"I know for a fact that he didn't. This dog probably came from the pound. At best. Although I wonder that any self-respecting dog pound would have accepted him in the first place, he's such an utter disgrace—not only to his breed, but to the entire species."

The dog looked mournfully up at Jackie, seeming to beg her indulgence for his appearance. The worry lines on his forehead deepened, and his jowls sagged.

Thalia Gilmore was going on with her tale. "I have been working with beagles for quite some time, but I thought the change would be interesting. My late husband always told me to be sure to trade up. I failed to follow his advice, and look what I'm stuck with."

"What's his name?" asked Jackie, stooping momentarily to stroke the dog's silky ears.

"Raphael. Idiotic name, but that's the name that came on his papers. His obviously forged papers."

"Well, sometimes even the best families have their black sheep," suggested Jackie. "I'm sure nobody could have predicted that he wouldn't be a champion."

"The person who sold him to me for five hundred dollars knew," was the stiff reply. "So much for you, Raphael," she said sternly to the dog. She looked at Jackie fiercely. "I saw you last weekend at the dog show."

Thalia Gilmore pronounced "weekend" with the emphasis on the second syllable—a distinctly British linguistic trick that Jackie had sometimes noticed in American women of a certain age and bearing. She wondered idly where it came from. Too many *Thin Man* movies, perhaps. Thalia Gilmore was certainly no Myrna Loy.

Jackie smiled. "My son and I have recently acquired a dog, and we're checking out all the angles."

"You're thinking of competing?"

"In a way. But last Sunday's performance convinced me that our Jake probably wouldn't make champion. So we thought we'd try obedience competition. He's a really good dog."

"What kind is he?"

"He's a German shepherd."

"Ah." Thalia Gilmore gave Jackie a knowing look. "The ringer."

"Ringer?"

"Yes, a ringer. If it's your shepherd that won the competition today. The one that tart was handling."

"Well—" began Jackie, stunned at the characterization of Sylvia Brown. Clearly, Thalia Gilmore spoke her mind on every subject.

"He's obviously a champion many times over, that dog of yours. Don't try to fool me, young lady. If this were an important competition, I'd have you hauled up before the judges' committee. What I'd like to know is where you got him."

"Actually, believe it or not, he just turned up on our doorstep one morning." Jackie was glad to be able to tell the truth. She didn't much like the suspicious way that Thalia Gilmore was looking at her. "He was hurt, so we took him in."

"I don't believe it," was the matter-of-fact reply. "Not that dog."

"It's true. His owner died, and he had wandered off. We found that much out later."

"Who was his owner? Not Lewis Perkins? He's the only one around here who breeds Alsatians that good."

"No, the man's name was Dugan."

"Dugan, Dugan," pondered Thalia Gilmore aloud. "Not the Dugans from Thornton Hill? I was at school with one of them. A very good family."

"No, I don't think so," said Jackie.

"Well, there really aren't any others." Clearly, Thalia Gilmore felt that if she didn't know a person, the person didn't exist. She harrumphed. "At any rate, I congratulate you. I was always taught to be a graceful loser." She glowered at poor Raphael, who by this time was sleeping soundly on the ground at her feet.

"Maybe he needs a friend," suggested Jackie. "You know, another basset hound. Give him something to look up to, someone to model himself after."

"Too late for that, I'm afraid. But I do plan to get another basset. Two, in fact. I've had my eye on them for three years, and they're the best around. I'm going to buy them, and I shall thus have my revenge on the swindler who sold me this bag of bones." She lifted an eyebrow at the snoozing Raphael. "Come on, you idiotic animal."

She yanked the dog's chain sharply, and Raphael stumbled to his feet. "Nice chatting with you." Thalia Gilmore hoisted Raphael into the back of her station wagon, climbed in the driver's seat, and slammed the door.

Jackie headed back over toward the benches, where the boys were waiting for her excitedly. Peter held up Jake's blue ribbon proudly.

"Whaddaya think about *that,* Mom?"

She tousled his reddish hair. "Just about what we expect of Jake, isn't it?"

"He's a pretty great dog," put in Isaac. "I just wish that everybody could really see him do his stuff."

"Yeah," agreed Peter warmly. "Like going after crooks."

"I think that might scare off some of the other contestants," suggested Jackie. "It's much better if people don't know everything that Jake can do. We'll keep that to ourselves, all right?"

"Yeah," said Isaac. "Not just anybody should know the power of Jake."

"The power of Jake is awesome," averred Peter.

Jackie, looking around for Sylvia Brown, was inclined to agree. She spotted Sylvia, at last. She had once more donned her baggy sweatsuit, and at the far end of the field she was engaged in conversation with a middle-aged man who had his back toward them. As Jackie watched, Sylvia pointed in their direction. The man turned, raised a hand to ward off the glare of the sunlight, and looked toward where Jackie and the boys were standing. Jackie felt an unaccountable shiver.

Undoubtedly the man was a stranger—yet as he turned his back on them once more, Jackie had a peculiar feeling that there was something familiar about him. The sensation made her nervous. She watched as the man continued his conversation with Sylvia, who nodded her head occasionally in Jackie's direction.

"Isaac," said Jackie at last, "will you do something for me?"

"Sure," said Isaac, who privately adored Peter's mother.

"Go and tell Sylvia Brown that we're ready to go. Peter and I will meet you at the car."

"Sure," said Isaac again. He sped away across the field, and Peter and Jackie gathered up the blankets and thermoses, then they and Jake headed for the Jeep. They had tarried a long time, accepting congratulations from the other contestants and making small talk; the Jeep was one of the last cars left in the parking lot.

On the way back to town, there was much exultation among the little party. Sylvia Brown looked particularly pleased with herself; Jackie, knowing how very well trained Jake was, was a bit surprised by the woman's attitude. Sylvia was smiling to herself, as though she had pulled off a difficult job.

CHAPTER 18

While Jake and company were enjoying their shining hour at the obedience competition, Michael McGowan was once more interviewing Ned Whiting. It was eleven on Saturday morning, and the precinct-house coffee, having spent three hours on the burner, had already acquired a stale, rotten flavor. McGowan sipped at it anyway, hardly noticing the acrid taste. There was something in the air this morning, a sense that progress would soon be made. But McGowan's face betrayed no hint of the anticipation he felt.

His men and women had talked to every member of the staff at the Senator Theater, where Whiting claimed to have been the night that his uncle was murdered. The Senator was one of the few movie houses in Palmer that hadn't converted itself into a "plex" of some sort. The Senator still had a balcony, and still employed ushers with flashlights to help people find seats in the dark. It was a poor movie house to select for an alibi. Much better to choose the Twelve-plex out at Running Brook Mall, on the road to Wardville. No one at the Senator could place him. What was more, the police had gotten a very lucky break. It was McGowan's hole card, to break down Whiting's alibi.

Today, McGowan was determined to get to the bottom of it. He had Whiting shown into an interrogation room,

instead of the office, when he arrived at eleven-fifteen. It
was a mean little room, windowless, and it had an unhappy, confessional atmosphere. There was nothing reassuring
about the pale blue-gray walls, or the scratched wood-
en table scarred by endless coffee-cup rings and cigarette
burns. The overhead lights were harsh and white. There
was nothing to look at, nothing to fix your eye on, except
the vacant blue-gray of the walls, and the eyes of the
interrogators. It was a room in which many detectives had
found a measure of success.

Sergeant Felix Cruz was stationed in an armchair in a
corner of the room, his bulk impressive in its immobility.
He had come to take notes, but there was also a tape
recorder on the table. The video recorder in the corner was
ready, if by chance they should hit pay dirt this morning.

After a few preliminaries, McGowan came to the point.
"I've had a full report from one of the managing partners
at Nash Brothers. You're in trouble, as I'm sure you know
by now. I don't think I have to remind you that this is a
murder investigation, and anything you say will go into the
official record of this interview. Sergeant Cruz has already
read you your rights. Is that accurate?"

"Yes." It came out a squeak, and Whiting tried again,
clearing his throat. "Yes, that's clear."

Whiting didn't look nearly as sure of himself this morning as he had on Thursday. McGowan knew that Nash
Brothers was on the point of dismissing him for failing to
keep accurate records. Johnny Shaw had been riding him
hard since Thursday. Evidently, he'd taken the wind out of
the young man's sails.

"All right then. I want to know exactly what kind of funny business was going on with your uncle's investments."

"Look," said Whiting. "Maybe I should come to the
point." He looked pale and haggard, as though he hadn't

slept. He gestured to the tape recorder. "Is that thing going?"

"What do you think? It's there for decoration?"

"I could lose my license as a broker."

"You should have thought about that sooner."

Whiting ran a hand through his dark hair, then drummed his fingers nervously on the table before him. His arms were long and skinny. He had dressed as though for the country club—in khaki pants and a bright blue polo shirt—but he had not managed to relax. "Maybe I should get a lawyer."

"You have the right, of course," said McGowan soothingly. "If you think you're ready to confess to your uncle's murder, I would strongly advise that you get yourself the best lawyer you can find. Generally speaking, lawyers are useful things when you're in a situation like this one."

Whiting gave him a contemptuous look, then appeared to make up his mind. "All right. Look—I swear I didn't kill him. I don't need a lawyer. You'll believe me, I promise."

"We'll see."

"I didn't kill him. But you're right that I haven't been exactly square with you. There was something—um— something about the portfolio that wasn't strictly within the rules."

"Such as the fact that you were stealing from him?"

"Oh, no," protested Whiting. "I never took a nickel from Uncle Mel. That is—"

"Not with his knowledge, you mean?"

"No, no. Not at all. It wasn't what I got out of it that was a little off. It was what he was investing."

"What do you mean?" This was unexpected.

"Look—can you imagine that a guy running a boarding school for dogs could salt away a million bucks? For starters, do you know how much he has to pay every year in taxes, insurance, and that kind of crap? He would barely have squeaked by. I know. I went over his books."

McGowan sat back. He was slightly relieved to think that it wasn't possible to make a million dollars in the dog business. Not legally, at least. "So?"

"So—well, when he came to me with a pile of money to invest, I got kind of curious."

"Yes?"

"I didn't ask him outright. He wasn't a very nice guy, and I didn't want to lose the chance of the commission on investing half a million."

"Very noble of you."

"But I couldn't figure out where he got it, because the Dog Academy seemed to have pretty accurate books, records of revenues and so forth. So I did a little snooping around one day at his house. At tax time, last year. I went over there to talk to him about capital gains, tax-free investments, and all that kind of stuff. He was doing his own taxes, and he didn't have the head for it. Doesn't know anything. So I was giving him advice."

"And?"

"Well, the first thing I noticed was that the revenues from the business were pretty good, like I said. But there shouldn't have been enough left over for him to have anything to invest. Let alone the forty grand he'd invested through Nash over the last year."

"What did you do?"

"Okay, I'm telling you." Whiting held up a hand, as though to quiet an insistent child. "He had some emergency out back, where the dog business was. Some old lady wanted to leave her poodle, and she hadn't paid her bill the last time, or something like that. I forget. Uncle Mel's manager came in to get him, because the old lady was being really pushy. He went out to handle it, and I used that opportunity to do a little digging around. I figured that if there was something off about the source of the money, I wanted to know all about it. It made me uncomfortable. I wanted to be ready to protect myself, if anyone came asking questions."

"A wise course, I suppose, under the circumstances," said McGowan sarcastically.

"Yeah, that's what I figured. So I went through all the books, which were right there, all together. Like I said, it was tax time, and I was helping him out. And there was this one ledger that had a bunch of names, dates, and amounts of money. Like that."

"What was suspicious about it?"

"The money never appeared anywhere else, in any of Uncle Mel's financial statements. So I figured it was cash that had been coming in somehow. And he was living off of that, paying the bills with it, and using his income from the business to invest. He would have been caught sooner or later—in fact I don't know quite how he got away with it for so long, unless he'd been doing everything in cash. He had used another broker up until about a year ago, when I went to work at Nash, and all I did was transfer some investments from one of the big New York investment houses. So I don't know, exactly. But it seemed off. Like one of those drawings, where it says 'What's wrong with this picture?' "

"Was it a lot of money?"

"It would have added up, that's for sure, because the book seemed to go back about ten or twelve years. A hundred bucks here, three hundred there—and all on the quiet."

Cruz was hastily making notes; he looked up at McGowan. The police search of the house had revealed no such ledger.

"Any idea where the money was coming from?"

"No. None at all."

"And you never asked your uncle about it?"

"Not for a long time. Then, right around Christmas last year, I found myself a little short of cash."

"Nice."

"Yeah, I always seem to run out right about that time. It's definitely a bummer."

"That wasn't what I meant, exactly. But never mind—go on."

"Huh? Well—anyway. I stopped by to ask Uncle Mel, kind of casually, if he could front me a grand or so. Just so I could get my family a couple of decent Christmas presents. Not for myself."

"No—definitely not for yourself."

"No. I mean, I was planning to go to Acapulco with this chick over New Year's, and I had bought the tickets on credit, so I was up to my limit on my Visa card, and for some reason I was real short of cash. But the loan wasn't for me."

"Believe me, I get the picture," said McGowan.

"So I figured that Uncle Mel could spare it. In cash. So I asked him for a loan, and he said he was all tapped out. So I said, almost without thinking about it, I said, 'What about the money in that ledger?' "

"What was his response?"

"At first he acted like he didn't hear me, or maybe didn't know what I was getting at or something. But I asked him again, and then he wanted to know how I knew about it, and I told him."

"And then?"

"Then he seemed to want to cut me in. I didn't pressure him or anything, I swear it. It was his idea."

"Uh-huh," said McGowan.

"And so he cut me in, but only through what I could earn by investing the money for him. We decided that if I could run a bigger pool of money for him than Nash knew about, put it in some offshore interests, then I could keep a bigger chunk of the investment commission. So the records in the file had to be a little off—because sooner or later somebody would have wanted to know about where the dough came from. So. That's why the portfolio was kind of a mess. It's not like I'm incompetent or anything. I did it on purpose."

Whiting seemed to think that the story demonstrated his skill. He had a satisfied look on his face.

"So you shared the pie with him for a while. And then you decided that Uncle Mel was just in the way of keeping the whole pie for yourself."

"No! No, I swear it. Look, it wasn't just Uncle Mel. He had a friend, a guy that was also getting this money, and I was helping him with his investments too."

"What was his name?"

"I don't know."

"Listen, little man," said McGowan contemptuously. "You're up the creek. The best thing you can do for yourself right now is to come clean, absolutely clean about the whole damn mess. You can be sure Uncle Mel's buddy, if there is such a creature, isn't going to go out on a limb to protect you. So spill it."

Whiting swallowed hard, glancing nervously from Mc-Gowan to Cruz and back again.

"I swear. I don't know."

McGowan and Cruz exchanged a look of tired disbelief.

"All right." McGowan returned his gaze to Whiting. "So you were running a pool of untraceable offshore investments for Uncle Melvin. Where did the money come from?"

"I swear I don't know. All I knew about it was what I found out that day last April."

"Okay. So. What do you think about the fact that not one of the employees at the Senator Theater can place you there for the ten o'clock show?"

Whiting shrugged. "It's a big theater."

McGowan nodded. "It's also rather unusual. That is to say, it's kind of an old-fashioned place. With a balcony, and ushers, and the whole works. Did you know that you can rent the whole movie theater for private parties?"

Whiting went pale, but recovered himself quickly. "No. No, I had no idea. Sounds like fun. Is it expensive?"

"Yeah. It's gonna cost you, buddy. Big time." McGowan permitted himself a small smile. "There was a private party at the Senator that night. *Thelma and Louise* was not showing—it was a party for a local group of vintage sci-fi buffs, a double bill of *The Thing* and *Attack of the Killer Tomatoes.*"

Whiting gulped.

"So you see," McGowan went on, "I think the time has come for you to tell me what you were doing that night."

"I think I want my lawyer."

"Call him."

Whiting sat perfectly still in his chair. He didn't speak for a full minute. Then he took a deep breath and seemed to reach a conclusion.

"All right. I did go to see Uncle Mel that night. But he was already dead. I got really scared, and just drove away."

"I don't buy it."

"No, honestly. Look, you've just got to believe me."

"Why?"

"Because!" It was the voice of a spoiled child. "Because I didn't do it, I swear." Whiting paused a moment, trying to recover his composure. "Listen. Uncle Mel had called me that day, said he wanted to talk to me."

"He had found out you were stealing from him."

"I *wasn't* stealing, I swear! There was plenty of dough to go around, the way it was coming in from him. No, he just wanted to ask me some questions about a mutual fund, and I told him I'd come over for a drink. His wife was away. She's really a drip."

"Cut the editorializing," said McGowan. "What happened?"

"Well, after work I went out with my buddies, just like I told you. We went to Charlie's Place, drank some brews, and I got a little lit. There was college basketball on the tube, and I forgot all about my appointment with Uncle Mel until the game was nearly over, about quarter of ten, maybe. I had told him I'd be there at nine. So I left."

"We've talked to one or two of your office mates. They say you sat in a booth by yourself most of the evening, staring at your beer. Then you left suddenly."

"Well, I was kind of worried. I'd made a few bad calls for another client, and I was trying to figure a way out of it. I was worrying that he might decide to cut his losses and go."

"So you were consumed with professional self-doubt. Then you took off like a bat out of hell to see your uncle. That was one way to solve the problem about the other client, am I right?"

"Hell, no." Whiting shook his head, like a teacher who cannot make a student understand a simple concept. "No, you have it all wrong. I just forgot I was supposed to go over there, and I didn't want him ticked off at me. So I hurried up."

"What time did you get there?"

"About ten."

"And?"

"I went in the front entrance—the driveway that goes up to the house, you know. Not the driveway that goes in through the Dog Academy entrance."

"And?"

"All the lights were on, so I knew he would still be up. That had been my big worry, because I knew he liked to go to bed real early, and I didn't want to wake him up."

"Right. Very considerate of you."

"You don't have to be so sarcastic," complained Whiting. "Anyway, I rang the doorbell, but there was no answer. The front door wasn't locked, so I went on in. He wasn't inside, so I figured he was out back with his basset hounds."

"So you went out back to look for him."

"Right. The lights were off in the kennels, but those two dogs of his were making a racket. So I called to him, but there was no answer."

"Were you worried?"

"To tell you the truth, I was feeling kind of spooked. I don't like to be outside in the dark at night. I went back into the kitchen, turned on the floodlight, and went back out toward the kennel. That was when I saw him."

"Where?"

"In the third dog run from the house. He was lying on his face. I went up for a closer look. I could tell that he was dead, because his legs and arms were all funny. You couldn't have them that way if they could feel anything. If you know what I mean. Plus, I could see this big chain around his neck, like a dog leash or something."

McGowan's description of the body tallied in every particular with the way the corpse had appeared to the police the following morning. There was no question that the young man had seen it.

"So you went inside to call a doctor, or the police. Am I right?"

"Yes. Well, I did think about that. I went back inside. And then I got to thinking that the police would suspect me.

I got really scared. So I just hopped in my car and drove and drove. I drove about forty miles out into the country, going really fast. Then I kind of came to my senses, and went back home. I figured I'd call the police in the morning, and say what had happened. But by the time the morning came I was scared again."

McGowan stood up, stretched, and glared at Whiting. "You're getting better at storytelling. Maybe you missed your calling. Maybe you should write fairy tales."

"It's the *truth!*" exclaimed Whiting. "I swear it! Look— all you have to do is check out his books. Then you'll have to believe me."

"I don't have to believe you, ever." McGowan gave Cruz a nod. They were through for the moment. "I'm not finished with you yet. But I have other things to attend to. Sergeant Cruz will type a statement for you to sign. You can wait in here until it's ready. We'll decide whether or not to charge you formally with obstruction of justice. For now. The rest will come later. Believe me, it will come."

Whiting slouched down in his chair. "Any chance of a cup of coffee while I wait?"

"Be careful what you wish for," McGowan replied. He nodded to Cruz. "Get him some coffee. That'll teach him."

CHAPTER 19

McGowan owed Jackie a telephone call. He had been giving her the brush-off for days now, and there was no reason for it, really, except the pressures of the job. Now that he had something more solid to go on, he was feeling a little bit like conversation.

The case was beginning to break wide open. McGowan had told Cruz, when they were finished taking Whiting's statement, that they were almost there. It would be a mere matter of days before the nephew decided to come clean with the whole truth. They needed to play their cards right, he told Cruz. But the two men were experienced at the game. They knew how to bluff their way past a full house with nothing but a pair of tens.

McGowan didn't bother to contain his satisfaction as he spoke to Jackie.

"I just wanted to say thank you for being patient with me. I think we've got our man, or we're close to it. Want to hear all about it?"

"Of course I do. That's really exciting, Michael."

McGowan filled Jackie in, from the beginning. He told her all about Whiting's claim that there was a secret fund of cash that necessitated the keeping of misleading records.

"I've never heard such a cock-and-bull story in my life," said McGowan contemptuously.

"You don't believe him, then."

"Of course not. He's been lying since the day he was born, that one, but he still hasn't got the hang of doing it very well. No. He was stealing his uncle blind, he was making unauthorized investments, or maybe he was failing to invest the money that his uncle asked him to invest. One way or another, he was playing fast and loose with half a million dollars."

"That's a *lot* of money, Michael."

"I know. I wish I were in the dog business."

"But does the story seem off-base to you?"

"Of course it does. He even admits he was there the night his uncle was killed."

"Oh! Tell me about it."

McGowan told her about the broken alibi and the way that Whiting had sulked over his beer at Charlie's Place before rushing off to his uncle's house. "Every time we get him down at the precinct house, he gets one step closer to telling us the truth. It's just a matter of time, now. But we've got him. We're sure of that."

"Congratulations," replied Jackie gently.

"Thanks. You know, now that I've had a few conversations with him, I'm surprised he had the brains to carry it out. At a guess, I'd say he has trouble tying his shoes."

"I didn't know murderers were supposed to be smart."

"He's what I'd call subnormally intelligent. He can read and write, I suppose, but about living in the world he has not got a clue. Don't know how he got a job at Nash Brothers."

"Connections," said Jackie. "His mother's uncle was one of the firm's founders. A long time ago."

"Now, how do you know that?"

"I don't know. That's just a part of Palmer history. Just one of the things you pick up on."

"Well, thank you for the history lesson," said McGowan gravely.

"You're welcome. What's your next step going to be?"

"We'll let him twist for a day or two, then get him back in here. He'll break."

"Well, let me know, won't you, how it turns out?"

"I will. And when we've got it all neatly packaged up, how about going to dinner with me?"

"Anytime," said Jackie, surprised at herself. She wasn't sure that going *out* to dinner with McGowan had the same innocence as letting him come around to their house for spaghetti every now and then. But it was too late to change her answer. She would just have to live with it. "Anytime," she repeated.

"I'm going to hold you to that."

As Jackie hung up the phone in her kitchen, she thought about what McGowan had told her. She wasn't surprised to hear that Whiting had been up to no good with his uncle's investments. There was an awful lot of that kind of thing going around these days. But she wasn't at all sure she bought the angle that he'd killed his uncle. Surely that was like killing the goose that laid the golden eggs? Besides, Jackie was convinced that there was something more to the whole affair. She was not satisfied that it boiled down to a question of money—that seemed too neat.

As she started to organize dinner for herself and Peter, she thought over everything she had seen and heard of the world that Mel Sweeten had moved in. Amy had been right, Jackie reflected, to characterize some of the participants as "disgustingly competitive." Not all were that way, of course—the man with the poodle, whom she had met on

Sunday, had been quite nice, despite being totally preoccupied with his little Serena. And this afternoon's excursion
had certainly been fun. Sylvia Brown had been positively
lighthearted. But a few of the people she had met were
in deadly earnest about their dogs. They seemed to be so
worried about winning that they didn't have the energy left
to enjoy themselves, much less enjoy their dogs.

Jackie was struck by a sudden idea.

"Peter!" she called upstairs.

"Yes, Mom?" Peter appeared at the top of the stairs.

"I have to go out on an errand. Why don't you give
Isaac a call and see if you can go over there for a while.
For supper, if they'll have you." Jackie knew that Peter
was welcome at Isaac's house at any time of day or night.
Isaac's mother was an easygoing woman, and she liked
Peter quite a lot. It was soon arranged.

Peter and Jackie and Jake headed for Isaac's house.
Jackie stopped in at the Cooks' house to say a quick hello
before she and Jake continued their course toward Linden
Lane, where Sylvia Brown lived in a small ground-floor
apartment of a townhouse. Jackie had dropped her off here
this afternoon, after Jake's triumph at the obedience competition.

With a start, Jackie realized that she had forgotten to
tell Michael McGowan about the obedience competition.
Not that Jake's blue ribbon would come as a surprise to
anyone—but still, McGowan deserved to be clued in. She
would tell him tomorrow—by which time she also hoped to
have some additional information for him about the case.

As she reached the door, she wondered briefly if she
was making a big mistake. She was convinced that Michael
McGowan was wrong about the nephew. No matter what
kind of a crook he was, she was utterly sure that there
was more to Mel Sweeten's death than mere money. There

was something about the way he had been killed that spoke
volumes. He had been choked to death by a dog collar, in
one of his own dog runs.

Surely the nephew wouldn't have been so picturesque?
Surely the manner of Sweeten's death pointed in one direction only?

But it was going to be difficult to prove, and in the
meantime, people might be at risk.

She buzzed Sylvia's doorbell, and the intercom clicked.

At six-fifteen that evening, a satisfied Michael McGowan
leaned back in his desk chair. His long, restless fingers
toyed with a rubber band, a habit he found both stimulating
to his mental processes and intimidating to suspects. He
kept his eyes firmly fixed on Cosmo Gordon, who had
dropped by to hear the news about the Sweeten case.

"I'm glad you came by," he said. "I'll tell you about the
Whiting kid in a minute. But in the meantime, I have good
news for you. We've found the gun that killed Matt Dugan."

Gordon looked gratified. "Where?"

"Not far from where he was killed. Looks like a mob
weapon. Serial number filed off, the whole bit. But the boys
and girls down in the ballistics lab say it's a make."

"Where did it come from?"

"That's the usual problem. But believe it or not, we may
have a break. You ever hear of a guy called Shorty, who
lives down on Front Street?"

"Sure. Gunrunner for the big boys."

"That's the one. Well, his kid got beat up kind of badly
last week. In the hospital and everything. So Shorty's been
on the horn to Cruz. Wants to talk about a few things."

"That's good."

"Yeah. Too bad about the kid. He lost an eye. But it may
be good for the city in the long run. There are times when

you just have to take the utilitarian viewpoint in this job."

"I'm with you," said Gordon. "There are times when the utilitarian viewpoint is the only one left."

"That too."

"Keep me posted, will you?"

"Of course. What did you get from the lab on that letter?"

"Nothing," said Gordon, shaking his head. "I didn't expect anything. But I'm worried about Nancy. She was at home with me the night that Dugan came over. The boys who sent me that letter know that Dugan came to the house. Probably they were having him watched. So they know Nancy was at home. But they have no way of knowing that she wasn't in the room when he began to talk about conspiracies."

"No." McGowan considered it for a bit. He saw an opening. "On the other hand, don't overestimate these guys. Remember that you're dealing with a fairly primitive bunch. They're right about at the level of the Cro-Magnon man in terms of social development."

McGowan was famous on the Palmer police force for his exceptionally enlightened view of modern society. Gordon, like others, was used to the young lieutenant's lectures on the equality of women. Unlike many others, Gordon was wholeheartedly in McGowan's camp. Their high regard for women, and their outspoken belief in equal pay for equal work, was one of the bonds that united them.

McGowan was warming to his theme. He smiled and shot his rubber band up at the overhead light, hitting the little metal hood that covered the bulb. His effort was rewarded with a resounding *ping!* He picked up another rubber band and continued his lecture.

"One aspect of the caveman personality is total insecurity around women, the need to subjugate them or keep them 'in their place,' wherever they think that is. By force, when necessary, or just by brutish emotional intimidation—by being nasty to them. Another aspect of that personality is, of course, the need to go around shooting people you don't like. But remember—it would never occur to these goons that you might want Nancy around when something important was being discussed. They whisper about things, or send their wives out of the room, unless the topic is food."

"Good point," replied Gordon, who had been following McGowan's reasoning. He grinned. "It hadn't occurred to me, but you're right, of course. They'd assume that Dugan and I would talk privately." There was genuine relief in his tone.

"There's one other thing you should know about the Dugan case," said McGowan. His tone was suddenly quite serious. "I got a call this afternoon from Cornelius Mitchell, the K-9 man."

"And?"

"And he had a call last week, from some man who wanted to know what had happened to Dugan's dog."

Gordon looked alarmed. This was just the kind of development he and McGowan had been worried about. Jackie's safety, they felt, depended on keeping Jake's identity a secret. They were sure that whoever had killed Dugan wanted to get to Jake—the dog had, after all, been a witness to his master's murder. And although he couldn't testify in a court of law, Jake was certainly capable of carrying out his own form of justice, if and when he got his chance. "Mitchell didn't tell the man anything, did he?"

"No. No, he has brains, that Mitchell. Even tried to get a trace on the call, while he pretended to look through the files. But whoever it was must have figured out what was going on, because he hung up."

"Have you told Jackie about it?"

McGowan shook his head. "I only just heard about it myself. I tried reaching her, but I guess she and Peter have gone out for the evening. There's no answer at her house."

"Well, you can tell her tomorrow. I'm sure that between now and then, she won't put herself at risk." He shot another rubber band at the light overhead. *Ping!*

CHAPTER 20

Sylvia Brown's voice came crackling through the intercom at her apartment door.

"Yes?"

"Sylvia, hi. It's Jackie. Got a minute?"

"Um—"

"Just a minute, really."

Jackie could hear a hurried movement. Then the front door buzzed, and Jackie and Jake went on into the vestibule.

"Hi," said Sylvia, opening her apartment door just a crack. "Oh. I see you've brought Jake."

"I wanted to talk to you," said Jackie.

"Well, I'm kind of busy right now." She looked pointedly at her watch. "I have to take a shower and get dressed. I'm going out a little later."

"It's important."

Sylvia looked thoughtful for a moment. "Okay." She swung the door wide to let Jackie and Jake pass.

Sylvia Brown's living room was small and sparsely furnished, but everything she had, thought Jackie, was in excellent taste. Sylvia clearly had an artistic streak, which manifested itself everywhere. Old crates, covered with bits of exotic-looking, hand-dyed cloth, served as end tables. There was a tiny fireplace, which had been fitted out a century ago for gas jets; the gingerbread wrought-iron grill in front of it had been painted brilliant colors. The curtains were colorful too, and the walls were hung with a series of watercolors—beach scenes, a stream, a farmhouse. There wasn't a hint of a basset hound among them.

Instinctively, and on purely aesthetic grounds, Jackie rejected the notion that Sylvia Brown had had an affair with Mel Sweeten. Sylvia Brown, Jackie thought, was probably capable of compromising herself, but not with a man who, in utter seriousness, had decorated his house with basset-hound lamps and basset-hound nut dishes. Jackie didn't see how it was possible; the two sensibilities would just not work together.

But she reminded herself that Amy Sweeten, as an art historian, presumably had a certain amount of taste as well. Maybe Mel Sweeten had been somehow devastatingly attractive to artistic women.

Sylvia, after greeting Jake with the enthusiasm due him, gestured Jackie to a chair and took a seat on the sofa. Jake found himself a comfortable spot halfway between the two women and put his nose down on his front paws.

"Okay," said Sylvia. "I guess it must be important, since you could have telephoned. I'm in the book."

Now that Jackie was here, she didn't quite know how to start. She had planned to start by talking about the rumors of the affair, but now that whole idea seemed an absurdity.

"Look—you'll probably think I'm crazy," Jackie began at last, "but I think maybe I can help you. If you're in a jam. Which I think you are."

"What makes you think so?"

"A lot of things. Mainly that you changed your mind and came with us today to the obedience competition. You said you needed practice with other breeds, but I think that was just an excuse."

"You're right," said Sylvia. Jackie waited, but the woman didn't elaborate. At last Jackie started up again.

"So. Okay, you wanted either to get something from me, or to talk to me. I figure that if you wanted to get something from me you would have worked on me, but you didn't. So that means you wanted to tell me something. The fact that you didn't manage to get it out means that it's hard to talk about. So I figure you're in a bind of some kind. And I thought maybe if I came over here and asked you, you'd talk."

Sylvia Brown laughed. "You should have been a psychologist. Or a detective."

"Am I right?"

"Yes, you are." Again, Sylvia grew silent. It began to look like Jackie would have to play Twenty Questions all evening. She decided to cut to the chase.

"Okay. You'd like to help the police get to the bottom of Mel Sweeten's murder. But you just don't know how to go about it. Am I right?"

Sylvia shook her long blond hair back out of her face and gave Jackie an appraising look. "How do you mean?"

"I mean this—that there was something going on."

"Hey, not you too! I am getting awfully tired of having people accuse me of carrying on." Sylvia looked disappointed. She had expected more from Jackie.

"I don't mean with Mel." Jackie looked her straight in the eye. "I don't believe you were having any kind of affair with him. But I do believe there was something up. Am I right?"

"Such as?"

"I couldn't really say. I'm here to get it from you. All I know is that Mel Sweeten was getting a lot of money from somewhere, and it wasn't from the Dog Academy. But the only thing he was interested in was dogs. So. Where was it coming from?"

Sylvia Brown looked uncomfortable. She hadn't expected the direct approach, clearly. She said nothing.

"You see," Jackie went on, "I don't really care about whatever little swindle is going on in the dog-show world. I doubt the police care, either. But Mel Sweeten was murdered, and I have a feeling that his killer might not want to stop there. So, since I like you, and think you have a lot of talent, I thought I'd try to talk some sense into you. Before it's too late. You may not even have to face a criminal charge, if you go to the police yourself. That's really all I came to say. I don't know if you've changed your mind about wanting to talk. But if you have, I suggest you call Michael McGowan and tell him what you know."

"I can't," said Sylvia in a quiet voice.

"Why not?"

"I'm terrified." She had gone suddenly ashen. "Don't you see? If anyone finds out I've gone to the police, I'll be next."

"If you help the police find the murderer, you won't have anything to worry about. Nothing at all."

"I doubt that." Sylvia Brown laughed.

"Why don't you try talking to me, then? I can't promise you anything—but I do sort of have an in with the police."

"So I've heard." Sylvia chuckled.

"What do you mean?"

"I mean that Dick Buzone sent you to talk to me so that he could figure out just how much the police knew. He says the detective is your boyfriend."

"He's wrong." Jackie felt a slow flush spread up her cheeks.

"What would you call him, then?" Sylvia was genuinely curious.

"He's a friend of the family."

"Oh."

For half a second, Jackie thought she detected a look of gratification on Sylvia's face. She felt a knot of anxiety beginning to form in her stomach, but she told herself sternly to keep her mind on the job. Being jealous of Sylvia could wait. What was important right now was Sylvia's safety.

"A good friend," Jackie added, not able to stop herself. "All right." Her tone was once again businesslike. "Why did Dick Buzone want to know about the police case?"

Sylvia sighed. "He had something going. He works as a judge, you know, at most of the big shows in the area."

"So I gathered. And I hear he isn't very popular with the owners and handlers."

"No," agreed Sylvia. "And with good reason. He takes bribes."

"So that's it," said Jackie. "I knew he was up to something."

"You did?"

"Well, he doesn't strike me as much of a dog person. I've seen him at two dog shows now, if you count today's competition, and he never really so much as glances at the dogs that are competing. It's as though he has his mind all made up at the beginning."

"I tried to tell him not to be so obvious about it," said Sylvia.

"All right. So he takes bribes. Big ones? Little ones? How does it work?"

"He puts out a little magazine. Maybe you've seen it— *The Canine Chronicle*."

Jackie nodded. "Yes, I've seen it. Articles on puppy cuts for poodles, and so forth."

"Right. Well, Dick has a system. He puts you on the mailing list for the magazine, and you pay a subscription rate of anywhere from ten bucks to a hundred bucks a copy. Depending. He can pretty much size up who can afford what."

"Whew!"

"I know. Ridiculous, isn't it? And subscribing for a year only puts you on the short list, for winning best of breed, or winning in a puppy class. To get on the best of show list, you have to have subscribed for two years. And after the two years, you have to pay five hundred dollars a year to stay on the list."

"Complicated. But what's the point of it all?"

"Oh, that's easy. The point is finishing your dog."

"Finishing."

"Getting your championship points. Because then you can breed your dog and sell the puppies for a lot of money. So you get your money back, in the long run."

"How many people are on the list?"

"Oh, I guess about fifty or sixty every year. Dick judges about twenty big shows, and he can give two awards in each show. There are always some subscribers left over, who have to resubscribe. It's quite a nice little racket."

Jackie grew thoughtful a moment. "I thought there was something odd about that newsletter," she said.

"Yeah. Well, it isn't just a one-way transaction all the time. Subscribers get to run advertisements if they want to, so sometimes it works out well for both sides."

"And what's your role, if you don't mind my asking?"

"Oh, nothing too big, really. Just to talk to people at shows, find out who might be willing to cough up the dough, and get back to Dick with their names."

"Set them up, kind of."

"Yeah, more or less." Sylvia was quiet a moment. "When I started out helping Dick, about three years ago, I thought he was just being friendly. He said he wanted to help me get to know all the right people, since I was thinking about becoming a professional handler. He gave me this long song and dance about how the dog-show circuit is really a people thing, more than a dog thing, and so it would be a good boost to my career if he helped me."

"And did he help you?"

"No. Well, yes, I suppose in a way he did, at first. But then he began to pump me for information about the people I was working for."

"Didn't you think that was suspicious?"

"Of course I did. But by that time I had figured out that he's a pretty nasty character. So I kept up the pretense, until I could find out what he was using the information for."

"And then?"

"Then I accused him of extorting money from people under the promise of gain, and that I'd go to the Am-DOG authorities. But he just laughed at me, and said I'd be totally out of work, because everyone would say that *I'd* been in it with him; that I'd been digging up all kinds of information on people. Which was true." She made a face. "He had me in a corner."

"Quite the prince, isn't he?" commented Jackie.

"Yeah. Prince of creeps. Well, I didn't have any hard evidence against him, and I figured that he had a point about my complicity. So I kept quiet, which wasn't right. But at least I had the integrity to cut him off."

"You stopped."

"Yeah, I refused to do any more work for him. Plus, I decided that I would ease out of the dog world into something a little less cutthroat. That's why I got my certification to teach aerobics."

Jackie could understand that it must have been a tough position for Sylvia. She could sympathize with the difficulty of the predicament, but she liked to think that in the same circumstances she would have blown the whistle—job or no job. It was hard to say.

"So," said Jackie thoughtfully, "pretty much all the championship points that he's awarded in the last three years have been as a direct result of bribes."

"Well, yes and no. Sometimes there's really not *that* much difference in conformation to the standard. Most judges have preferences; Dick just preferred those who paid for the honor."

"I don't think I know what you mean," replied Jackie.

"Okay, look. Say you have a dog show, and there are five winners competing for best in show. They've all won best of breed, already, because that's the way a dog show works."

"Right," said Jackie, who had gathered as much in her brief visit to the show at the armory last Sunday.

"So if the prize goes to, say, Jake here, instead of to a toy poodle, it's really got a lot to do with how much the judges like shepherds in general, as compared to toy poodles."

"I see."

"People who enter dog shows choose their judges carefully. Because it's really hard, if your dog wins best of breed, and then he gets shot down for best in show just because the judge doesn't like his kind. But that has been known to happen, believe me."

"It's subjective."

"Exactly. So—Dick's choices are subjective too. How much everyone has paid him, and whether he wants to make them go on paying and paying. There are a few people whose money he's been taking for thirteen years, and still he's never given them best in show."

"Why do they keep trying?"

"God only knows," replied Sylvia. "You would think that they would figure out that he'd never come through."

Jackie grew thoughtful. "Where did Mel Sweeten figure into all of this?"

"Oh—he was taking about half the cut. Supposedly the whole scheme was his idea. At least that's what Dick told me, although I never am quite sure how much of what Dick says to believe."

Jackie nodded. It fit with what Michael had told her this afternoon about the nephew and the mysterious income.

"Who else knew about their little game?"

"Besides me?" Sylvia shook her head. "Nobody."

"Are you sure?"

"Positive. They thought it was a scream. Mel especially, because Dick was always making his bassets champions. Then Mel would give him a little kickback on the stud fee, or something."

"What a pair."

"I know. They were pretty awful."

"Tell me, Sylvia," Jackie began, but the other woman cut her off.

"Let me guess. You heard the rumors about me and Mel. You also know I was handling his bassets. Now you know that I knew he was a crook. You want to know what was going on. Right?"

"Right," said Jackie.

"Not much. Just this: I adore Fred and Karen. I've been working with them, and placing Karen's puppies, and finding mates for Fred, for three years—and I'm just crazy about them. That's all."

For some reason, Jackie found this explanation utterly

compelling. It answered every question, it left no loose ends, no "what-ifs" lying about.

Now that she had her answers about Sylvia Brown, Jackie decided it was high time to confront the murderer of Mel Sweeten. She thanked Sylvia for her time and took her leave, considering, on her way home, what would be the best way to approach the next person on her list.

The very first thing to do was to call Michael McGowan and tell him what her plan was. Jake or no Jake, she didn't relish the idea of a confrontation without knowing that help would soon be on the way.

CHAPTER 21

"Wait a second, Jackie. Hold on, would you? Just let me turn down the volume so I can hear you." Michael McGowan had just settled himself in front of the television. The Lakers were playing the Celtics. The beer was cold, the pretzels were crisp, and he was exhausted. What he clearly did not want was to talk about the murder of Mel Sweeten.

"But, Michael, there's no time to lose. I tell you that Dick Buzone's life is in danger."

He caught the end of this frantic statement as he returned to the telephone. One of these days, McGowan often vowed, he would buy a new television with remote control. But on a lieutenant's salary, after alimony payments every month, there was never enough left over for that dream machine.

"Okay," he said. "Start again."

Jackie repeated her assertion.

"You're not serious."

"Of course I am. Listen." She told him about her visit to Sylvia Brown's apartment. "Michael, that kid Whiting was telling you the truth. There was a slush fund. It was the subscription list for that stupid newsletter."

McGowan could have kicked himself. Jackie had pestered him and pestered him about that subscription list, and he had dismissed everything she said. Now it looked like he had been a little too high-and-mighty.

Worse yet, it looked like his case against Ned Whiting would collapse. If there had been a slush fund, then maybe there was truth in his account of having found his uncle dead. "Just what I needed," said McGowan ungratefully. "I'm back at square one."

"No, you're not. Michael, I think I know who killed Mel Sweeten."

"Do tell."

So Jackie told, and told him her reasons for thinking so. Then she told him what she thought they ought to do about it. She had a plan, but she needed his help. Would he make one little telephone call for her?

McGowan listened to her plan in amazed silence. While he had been concentrating on Ned Whiting, Jackie Walsh had seen clear through to the bottom of the problem. Feeling slightly sheepish, he agreed to her plan, with one proviso— that she would take Jake with her.

"Of course I will. What, you think I'm crazy or something? I'm not going all the way out there to face a murderer without my bodyguard."

"I'll meet you there in twenty-five minutes," said McGowan.

In less than that time, in twenty minutes, Jackie and Jake had arrived at Mel Sweeten's Dog Academy. The lights were blazing in the house; Jackie had expected Amy to be at home. She had the feeling that Amy was almost always at home, at least when the library was shut.

She and Jake made their way up the darkened path, past Fred and Karen, who set about howling magnificently at the intruders. That was what Jackie wanted—she wanted to get them stirred up, the way they had been the night that Mel Sweeten was killed.

She wanted to hear how they responded to the presence of something that they were afraid of. Tonight, it was Jake, who gave off immense vibes of power and authority, even in the dark, even on territory that was clearly not his own.

That night, it had been Mel Sweeten's murderer—a person that the bassets loathed and feared.

As Jackie and Jake arrived at the front door, another car pulled up in the driveway. Jackie recognized the station wagon that Thalia Gilmore had been driving that morning at the obedience competition. Jackie didn't wait for Thalia, but knocked straightaway at the front door.

Amy answered in less than five seconds. She must have been pacing in the hallway.

"Jackie!" she said in stunned surprise. "What are you doing here?"

"May I come in?"

"Um, sure. Do you mind leaving your dog outside?"

Thalia Gilmore arrived huffing and puffing. "What is all this about?" she demanded.

"It's about the night that Mel Sweeten was murdered," said Jackie quietly. "And no, Amy, I'd prefer to bring Jake inside with me. If it's all the same to you."

Amy Sweeten, looking mystified, shrugged her shoulders and led the way into the living room, with the two other women and Jake on her heels.

"What do you mean it's about that night?" Thalia Gilmore bellowed. "I have never heard anything so absurd in my life." She turned to give Amy an indignant stare. "Who *is* this woman that you let her push you around, Mrs. Sweeten?"

"She's a colleague," replied Amy in a level voice. She was regarding Jackie warily. "She's a member of the faculty at Rodgers University."

"Well, what on earth is she doing here, at this time of night, with her dog?"

"I'm not sure," replied Amy in a faint voice.

"I'm here conducting a little experiment," said Jackie. "And I needed your help, Mrs. Gilmore."

"My help? This is absurd. It's outrageous. I came here to ask Mrs. Sweeten a question or two, not to play some silly game with you. I'm going *straight* home."

"I really wish you'd stay," Jackie replied. "You're the only person who can help us."

"How can I *possibly* help you, child?"

"Mrs. Gilmore, you were here that night."

"Of course I was. Everyone knows that. I'm a member of the executive committee of the Greater Palmer Dog Fanciers Association."

"You remember, don't you, the noise that the dogs made in the middle of your meeting?"

"I most certainly do. A horrid racket, perfectly dreadful. Mel had to go outside and quiet them down."

"When he returned to the room, how did he look?"

"Shaken. But I thought—that is to say, I had rather been hoping that he had decided to confess his treachery to me. He had poisoned my Clematis, down in Philadelphia, made her terribly ill so that she couldn't compete. That was the day she was supposed to have won best in show too."

Thalia Gilmore looked suddenly alarmed. "I mean to say—"

"I know exactly what you mean to say, Mrs. Gilmore. You mean to say that you had been one of Dick Buzone's 'subscribers' for many years, and he had put you off, continually. But with Clematis you really thought you had a chance of winning, and then she was ill."

"That's right. And one of Karen's pups, well not a pup any longer, she's two or three by now—anyway, one of

Mel's dogs, in effect, won not only best in the Hound class but also won best of show. It was *terribly* unfair. And Mel Sweeten ought to have been shot for doing such a thing." The blood drained from Thalia Gilmore's face as she realized her gaffe. "Oh, I'm so *dreadfully* sorry, Mrs. Sweeten, I didn't mean—"

"Don't give it a thought, Mrs. Gilmore," Amy replied. "Would anyone like a cup of tea or anything? Or maybe just tell me why you're here."

"Mrs. Gilmore wants to buy Fred and Karen, Amy." She gave Thalia Gilmore a look; and that large lady, for once, kept her mouth shut. Jackie went on. "I told her that you were interested in her offer, but I thought it was a little low. She has agreed to pay five thousand for the pair of them."

"Great," said Amy. "The sooner the better. I can use the money, and all of our cash is tied up in probate. Everything was in Mel's name." She smiled her pale little smile.

"Well, my dear," said Thalia Gilmore, rising magnificently to the occasion, "I have brought my checkbook with me. I'm all ready to go."

"The only thing is," Jackie interrupted, with a hard, even stare at the astonished Thalia Gilmore, "that Mrs. Gilmore would like to take a look at the dogs before she writes the check."

"I certainly would. My late husband always told me that I ought to look before I leapt. He was a very wise man." She addressed Amy. "Would you do me the kindness, my dear, of bringing the dogs inside so that I can take one last look at them before I sign on the dotted line?"

"Sure," said Amy. "Jackie, you know more about dogs than I do. Would you let them in? And I'll make a pot of tea."

"I think I'd better stay here with Jake, Amy. I'm the only one in this room who can control him, and I would hate for anything to happen to Fred and Karen. Just go get them and bring them in the kitchen. Then I'll take Jake out."

Amy Sweeten, looking visibly reluctant, complied.

A minute passed. And then, with a noise like something out of the nether world, Fred and Karen set up their alarm call. Thalia Gilmore gave Jackie a questioning look, but didn't say a word.

In another minute or two, Amy had come back inside.

"They're really stubborn," she said lamely. "You'd better go on out and have a look for yourself, Mrs. Gilmore."

"They hate you, don't they, Amy?" asked Jackie.

"They're just stupid dogs. Go on outside, Mrs. Gilmore. They're right in their pen."

"They hate you and they fear you," said Jackie in a flat, calm, implacable voice. She turned to Thalia Gilmore. "Is that the noise they made the night that you were here?"

"Yes," said Thalia Gilmore. "I'd never heard anything like it. Certainly not out of Fred and Karen. But that was it."

Jackie returned her gaze to Amy, who was looking stricken. "They hate you and they fear you, Amy, because you have always hated them," said Jackie, her voice quiet and calm. "And because you murdered their friend. They despise you and revile you, and call out in a wild voice whenever you come near. Isn't that so, Amy?"

Amy Sweeten had gone a pale, dead gray. She was breathing rapidly, in shallow little breaths, and staring hard at Jackie. Finally she found the breath to speak.

"No. You're wrong."

"I'm not wrong. If I'm wrong, go and get those dogs for me, and bring them inside. They'll tell you who's right and who's wrong."

"No, I can't," said Amy, her eyes wild. "They're just stupid dogs."

"Go and get them," repeated Jackie.

"I can't. I can't." Amy's voice broke, and her thin little body was racked with sobs. "I can't, I can't, I can't. They'll kill me."

"Who will?" persisted Jackie in the same low, level voice. "Who will kill you?"

"They will, they'll kill me, they'll tear me apart. They were there!" She sank onto the sofa, her voice hysterical. "They know!"

"What do the bassets know, Amy?"

"They know that I killed Mel!" Now Amy's whole body shook as if she were sobbing, but her eyes were dry. Jackie went quickly and quietly to the front door and opened it. Michael McGowan was there. Jackie nodded and led him in.

Amy was hugging her knees to her chest, rocking back and forth on the sofa, sobbing great huge dry sobs. "I killed him! I killed him!" she cried out, again and again. "I did it, and the bassets know! The bassets know!"

CHAPTER 22

The following day, Jackie invited Sylvia Brown and Thalia Gilmore to lunch, and refused to take no for an answer. Sylvia promised to give all the statements necessary to the police about the extortion racket. McGowan had phoned her that morning, and he seemed to feel that no charges would be pressed against her.

Thalia, of course, knew the reason for being summoned to Jackie's. She had totally recovered her magnificent aplomb, and was reveling in her important role of the evening before. Sylvia was amazed at the tale. Michael McGowan arrived just in time for dessert, to hear Thalia Gilmore doing quite a passable imitation of Fred's and Karen's wailing. The noise roused Jake, who had been drowsing under the kitchen table. Peter and Isaac, playing Game Boy in the den, emerged to find out what all the noise was about.

McGowan settled down familiarly at the kitchen table.

"We've got the full confession. You were absolutely right, Jackie. The woman is crazy."

"Who's crazy, Mom?"

"A lady who murdered her husband, sweetie."

"And you caught the murderer?" Peter beamed and poked Isaac in the ribs. That made it two to zero. Isaac's mother hadn't caught any murderers.

"Jake and I did, honey. I'll tell you all about it. Do us a favor, though, and run along. Okay?"

Peter knew that his mother only sent him out of the room when he was likely to get a better version of the story later—when she didn't have to be polite in front of strangers. So he dragged the protesting Isaac back to the den. "It's better this way, I promise," said Peter. "You can stay for supper."

"Okay."

The group in the kitchen listened fascinated as McGowan told them the whole story. "She turned up at the Dog Academy at about eight o'clock. She was going to poison the bassets. But as you know, they made a terrible racket. Mel Sweeten came out of the house; he knew that the dogs only made that kind of noise when they were really upset about something."

"That's true," put in Sylvia, who knew Fred and Karen better than anyone else, except Mel Sweeten. "They always made that noise when Amy was anywhere around. They just *hated* her."

"So she hid in the bushes behind the dog runs, while Mel quieted the dogs down. Apparently he knew that she must be there. He called her name a couple of times, but got no answer. So he went back inside."

"No *wonder* he looked so upset," said Thalia Gilmore.

"He had suspected Amy of trying to poison the dogs once before," put in Sylvia. "But he couldn't prove it. All he knew was that she was insanely jealous of them."

"What did she do—jump him when he came back outside?" asked Jackie.

"Not exactly. She says Mel came out and looked around a little bit. Then he sat down, and after a while he fell asleep. I suppose he was trying to stand guard over the dogs or something, in case she was still around." McGowan shook his head. "He knew how much she resented them. Once he was asleep, she had her opportunity. I don't know if he was even aware of what was happening."

"You can't really blame the poor thing for being jealous," said Thalia. "He was a total nut about those dogs. And as far as I could tell, he never gave her a thought."

"You're wrong about that," said Sylvia. "He was terribly worried about her mental condition. She apparently had decided to do her doctoral thesis on dogs in art, which the university thought was a bad idea. But she was persisting, finding every portrait that had ever been done of a dog, finding every casual dog that ever appeared in a painting. She was hunting for bassets, but they were scarce. It was really spooky. Mel was wondering how to get help for her."

"You didn't help things, my dear," reproved Thalia Gilmore. "Just look at you."

"I can't help the way I look, Mrs. Gilmore. Mel and I were never anything but friends. And even not such good friends toward the end. My real friends in the dog-show circuit were Fred and Karen."

"Hmph," said Thalia Gilmore.

"What about the nightgown, Michael?" asked Jackie.

"There never was any nightgown. If we'd gotten around to it, we'd have found out that her story didn't check out. She admitted to me in her confession this morning that she had made that whole thing up. Oh, she *was* convinced he was fooling around, but she had no evidence. She just decided to focus her accusations on Sylvia. To cast suspicion around."

Jackie shivered. "In a way, I feel sorry for her. But I feel sorry for Mel too. I'll bet she was constantly on his back, spying on him. . . . There's something so ugly about a marriage without any love or trust."

"Speaking of spies, Jackie," said Sylvia, "there was a guy at the obedience competition the other day asking me all kinds of questions about Jake. And about you."

McGowan and Jackie exchanged a look. "Why?" asked the detective.

Sylvia shrugged. "Got me. I told him that Jake belonged to Jackie, because he could have found that out from anyone. Then he kind of took off. Hey, what's it all about?" She had noticed the anxious look in McGowan's eyes.

He explained briefly the circumstances of Jake's arrival.

"He's a *police* dog?" Sylvia was disbelieving. Then she nodded. "I wondered where he'd learned his stuff."

"Please don't mention it to anyone, under any circumstances," cautioned McGowan. "Jackie and Peter aren't really safe until we can get the guy who murdered Matt Dugan. And the people he works for."

"Well," said Sylvia, "if that's your next case, maybe I can help. Here." She fished in her wallet and dug out a scrap of paper. "This is the license of the car that guy was driving yesterday."

She smiled at the astonished group. "My father always taught me to be on the lookout for creeps. I think I'm finally learning to follow his advice." She handed the slip of paper to Jackie. "I think this will be your next case. Yours and Jake's."

Jake, from under the kitchen table, let out a low *woof*. He was evidently ready to solve his own mystery.